Secret Meeting

Also by Jean Ure

Passion Flower
Pumpkin Pie
Shrinking Violet
Boys on the Brain
Skinny Melon and Me
Becky Bananas, This is Your Life!
Fruit and Nutcase
The Secret Life of Sally Tomato*
Family Fan Club
Collins Book of Ballet and Dance Stories (ed.)

and for younger readers

Dazzling Danny
Daisy May
Monster in the Mirror

*Also available on tape, read by John Pickard

Secret Meeting

JEAN URE

Illustrated by Karen Donnelly

HarperCollins *Children's Books*

For Chris and Joan,
with love and respect

CAMDEN LIBRARIES

First published in Great Britain by HarperCollins *Children's Books* 2004
HarperCollins *Children's Books* is a division of HarperCollins*Publishers* Ltd,
77-85 Fulham Palace Road, Hammersmith,
London W6 8JB

The HarperCollins *Children's Books* website address is
www.harpercollinschildrensbooks.co.uk

2

Text copyright © Jean Ure 2004
Illustrations © Karen Donnelly 2004

ISBN 0 00 715620 0

The author and illustrator assert the moral right to be
identified as the author and illustrator of the work.

Printed and bound in England by
Clays Ltd, St Ives plc

one

MY FRIEND ANNIE is completely bonkers. Loopy, wacko. Seriously *doo*lally, as my nan would say. She does the craziest things! Like in biology, one time, we were supposed to be dissecting plums, and when Miss Andrews said, "Annabel Watson, where is your plum?" Annie said, "Oops, sorry, miss! I ate it."

"*Ate* it?" said Miss Andrews. "Ate your *plum*?"

She couldn't believe it! I could, 'cos I know Annie. She drank some paint water once, when we were in juniors. She said it looked so pretty, like pink lemonade.

Some people think she does it to show off, but it's not that at all. She just happens to be a very zany sort of person. I, on the other hand, am desperately sensible and boring. I would never do anything silly, if it weren't for Annie. She is always getting us into hot water! The only times I ever have my name in the order mark book are when Annie's told me to do something and I've gone and done it, even though I know it means trouble. Like, for instance, hiding ourselves in the stationery cupboard when we should have been outside playing hockey. I knew it would end in disaster. I only did it 'cos I hate hockey – well, and because Annie said it would be fun. What she didn't realise was that Mrs Gibson, our head teacher, was due to take a special sixth form study group in our classroom. With us still in the cupboard!!!

Mrs Gibson was quite surprised when someone opened the cupboard door and we fell out. We were quite surprised, ourselves.

That was *two* order marks. One for missing hockey, and one for damaging school property (trampling on the stationery).

Then there was the time she decided – Annie, I mean – that we should go to school wearing birds' nests in our hair. She'd found these old nests in her garden and she said, "Think how cool it would look! We could start a new fashion." She perched one on her head and it sat there like a little cap, really sweet, with tiny bits of twig and feather sticking out, so I did the same, and we went into assembly like it, and people kept looking at us and giggling, until all of a sudden this *thing*, this horrible maggoty *thing*, started to crawl out of Annie's nest and slither down the side of her face, and the girl next to her screeched out, really loud, like she was being attacked by a herd of man-eating slugs.

I screeched, too, but in a more strangulated way, and tore my nest off and threw it on the floor, which started a kind of mini stampede and brought the assembly to a standstill.

We didn't actually get order marks for that, but Mrs Gibson told us that we were behaving childishly and irresponsibly, adding, "I'm surprised at *you*, Megan." Later on, at Parents' Evening, she told Mum that I was too easily influenced.

"She lets herself be led astray."

She meant, of course, by Annie. If it weren't for Annie I'd probably be the goodest person in the whole of our class! I might even win prizes for "Best Behaviour" or "Hardest Working". To which all I can say is *yuck*. I'd rather have order marks and be led astray! I can't imagine not being friends with Annie. Even Mum admits that there is nothing malicious about her. She may have these wild and wacky ideas that get us into trouble, but she is warm, and funny, and generous, and is always making me laugh.

Last term she gave me this card. It was really beautiful, all decorated with little teensy pictures of flowers and animals that she'd done herself.

Inside it said:

> TWELVE TODAY!
> HIP HIP HOORAY!
> HAPPY BIRTHDAY!

"What's this for?" I said.

Annie beamed and replied, "For your birthday."

But my birthday wasn't for another whole week! I couldn't believe that my very best friend in all the world had forgotten when my birthday was.

"It's not till the end of the month," I said. "Twenty-eighth of April!"

"I know," said Annie. "But I wanted you to have it now. I'll do you another one for your real birthday!"

"You're mad," I said. "Who gives people birthday cards when it's not their birthday?"

Annie giggled and said, "I do!" And then she said that maybe it was an *un*birthday card, and she started singing "Happy unbirthday to *you*, happy unbirthday to *you*, happy un*birth*day, dear Mc-gan, happy unbirthday to *you*!"

I put my hands over my ears and begged her to stop. Annie has a voice like a screech owl. Really painful! Not that mine is much better.

Mum says it sounds like a gnat, buzzing to itself in a bottle. But it is not as loud as Annie's. And I wasn't the one singing happy unbirthday!

"I'm going to give you a really good birthday present," said Annie. "A *really* good one."

I said, "What?"

Annie said she hadn't yet decided, and even if she had she wouldn't tell me. "But it's going to be something you'll really, really like!"

"What I would really really like," I said, "is the latest Harriet Chance."

I'm sure I don't need to tell anyone who Harriet Chance is. She is just my all-time mega favourite author is all! Mine and about fifty million others. But I am her number-one fan! I have read almost every single book she's ever written. Which is *a lot of books*. Fifty-one, to be exact; I looked it up on one of the computers in our school library. Thirty-four of them are on the shelf in my bedroom. I call them my Harriet Chance Collection. I couldn't wait to get my hands on the latest one!

"It's called *Scarlet Feather*," I said. "Scarlet is this girl who goes to stay with her nan 'cos—"

Annie made an exaggerated groaning noise. She quite likes Harriet Chance, she is just not the huge fan that I am.

"Well, anyway," I said, "it's all right, I wouldn't expect you to get it for me. It's in hardback and costs simply loads." I heaved a sigh. Very dramatic. "I'll just have to wait till the paperback comes out."

"Why?" said Annie. "You can get it with your book tokens. You know you'll have lots."

It's true, I always ask for book tokens when it comes to my birthday or Christmas. Annie thinks it is just sooo boring.

"You get it with your book tokens," she said, "and I'll

think of something else... I'll think of something far more exciting!"

I said, "Nothing could be more exciting than a new Harriet Chance."

"Oh, no?" said Annie. "Wanna bet? I'll find something, don't you worry!"

"Not like last time," I begged.

For my last birthday she'd given me this long blonde wig and some spooky black eyelashes and plastic fingernails, "to make you look glamorous!" I did look glamorous. It was brilliant! Mum didn't approve, of course, but I sometimes think that my mum is just a tiny bit old-fashioned. Certainly compared to Annie's. But she didn't really mind, she let me dress up for my birthday party and paint the plastic fingernails purple. Unfortunately, I turned out to be allergic to the glue that stuck the eyelashes on, and next morning when I woke up my eyes were all swollen like footballs.

It wasn't Annie's fault, but I had to go to the doctor and get some special cream and couldn't leave the house for three whole days. Well, I could have done, but I was too embarrassed. This is the sort of thing that just always, somehow, seems to happen with Annie.

"I don't want more eyelashes!" I said.

"Not going to get more eyelashes."

"I don't want anything with *glue*."

"It won't be anything with glue! I'm going to think of something really special... hey!" Annie tiptoed over to the door (we were in her bedroom at the time) and peered out. "D'you want to go on the computer?"

I hesitated. "You mean... go to that site you told me about?"

Slowly, I shook my head. I would have liked to, I would *really* have liked to, but I'd promised Mum.

"When you're round at Annie's, I don't want you playing with that computer. I want you to give me your word!"

When Mum said "playing with the computer", what she really meant was chatrooms. She'd heard all these stories about middle-aged men pretending to be young boys, and girls going off to meet them, and they had scared her. They scared me a bit, too, though as I said to Mum, "I wouldn't ever go and *meet* anyone." Mum said she didn't care, she wanted me to promise her.

I do sometimes think Mum tends to fuss more than other people's mums. I suppose it is because I am all she has got, now that Nan is in a home. I don't remember what it was like when Dad was with us; I was too young. Perhaps it was after he left that Mum got nervous. Well, not nervous, exactly, but not wanting me to do things like go into chatrooms. Annie's mum and dad let her do pretty well whatever she wants. She even had her own computer in her bedroom. I didn't have a computer at all! Mum had always promised me one for when I was fourteen. She said we'd find the money somehow. I didn't really mind not having one. Not usually, I didn't. Not when I had all my Harriet Chances to read! Just now and again I thought that it would be fun and wished Mum didn't have to "count every penny". But I knew it was a worry for her.

"Megs?" Annie was standing poised, with one finger on the mouse. She had this impish grin on her face. "Shall I?"

I muttered, "You know I'm not allowed into chatrooms."

"'Tisn't a chatroom!" said Annie. "It's a *book*room. Wouldn't go into a *chat*room." She looked at me reproachfully. "I know you're not allowed into *chat*rooms."

I was still doubtful. "So what's the difference?"

"This is for *bookworms*," said Annie. "You just talk about books, and say which ones you like, and write reviews and stuff. Honestly, you'd love it! It's your sort of thing."

It *was* my sort of thing; that was what made it so tempting. But I was quite surprised at Annie visiting a chatroom for bookworms. It's not her sort of thing at all! I mean, she does read, but only 'cos I do. I don't think, probably, that she'd bother with it if it weren't for me.

"What books do you talk about?" I said.

"Oh! Harriet Chance. Everyone talks about Harriet Chance. I'm only doing it," said Annie, "'cos of this project thing."

She meant our holiday task for English. We all had to review one of our favourite books and write a bit about the author. There are no prizes for guessing who I was going to do... Harriet Chance! I just hoped Annie didn't think she was going to do her, too.

I said this to her, and she said, "Well, I won't if you don't want me to, but who else could I do if I didn't do her?"

"Anyone!" I said. "J.K. Rowling."

"I can't do J.K. Rowling! *Harry Potter*'s too long."

"So do something short... do *Winnie the Pooh*."

"Oh. Yes." She brightened. "I could do that, couldn't I? I love *Winnie the Pooh*!" She then added that even if *she* didn't do Harriet Chance, half the rest of the class probably would. "There's more people that talk about her books than almost anyone else."

"That's because she's a totally brilliant writer," I said.

"Yes, and it's why you ought to visit the bookroom, so you can see for yourself," said Annie. "Look, it's ever so easy, all I have to do is just—"

"*Annie Watson, you fat little scumbag, I hope you're obeying the rules?*"

Annie dropped the mouse and spun round, guiltily.

It
was
her
sister,
Rachel,
who'd
crept up
the stairs
without our
hearing.
Rachel is four years older
than Annie and me. She
always house-sits when it's
school holidays and her mum
and dad are at work.

"I saw you!" she said. "You
were going to use that
computer!"

"I'm allowed!" shrieked Annie.

"You're not allowed to go on the Net.
Not when Megan's here. You know that
perfectly well."

"Wasn't going to go on the Net," said Annie.

"So what were you going to do?"

"I was going to... write something. For school."

"Like what?"

"Our project," said Annie. "F'r English."

"*Fringlish?*"

"Book reviews!" roared Annie.

Rachel narrowed her eyes. They are bright green, like a cat's, and very beautiful. Rachel herself is rather beautiful. While Annie is little and plump, Rachel is tall and slim. This is because of all the work-outs she does, and the games of hockey that she plays (instead of sitting in the stationery cupboard, trampling on the stationery).

They both have black hair, but Rachel's is thick and straight, like a shiny satin waterfall, while Annie's is all mad and messy, with some bits curling in one direction and some bits curling in another.

I have often thought that I should like to have a brother or sister, if my dad hadn't gone and left us before he and Mum could get round to it, but I'm not sure that I'd want a sister like Rachel. She is just *sooo* superior. Like she reckons anyone in Year Seven is simply beneath her notice. Like small crawling things in the grass; just too bad if they get trodden on. On the other hand she *was* supposed to be supervising us, so maybe it's not surprising if she came across a bit bossy.

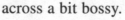

"If you can't be trusted," she said, "you can go downstairs."

"We're not *doing* anything," said Annie.

"I still think it would be better if you went downstairs."

"We don't want to go downstairs! We're happy up here."

"Yes, well, I'm not happy with you up here! I'm the one that'll catch it if you do something you're not supposed to."

Annie flounced, and huffed, but I knew, really, that Rachel was right. Another minute and I might have given way to temptation. I had to admit that I didn't personally see anything so wrong in visiting a chatroom for bookworms; I mean you'd think it would be classed as educational, but I had given Mum my word. It was the only reason she let me go round to Annie's. I knew she wasn't terribly happy about it, because of Annie having her own computer and her mum and dad being a bit what Mum calls *lax*; but Mum couldn't always get time off in school holidays.

"I just have to trust you," she said.

It was probably all for the best that Rachel had stepped in. I don't *think* I would have been tempted, because in spite of what Mrs Gibson and Mum believe,

I do quite often stand up to Annie. Not if it's just something daft that she wants us to do, but if it's something I actually think is wrong. Like one time she showed me a packet of cigarettes she'd found and wanted us to try smoking one. I didn't do it because I think smoking cigarettes is just too gross. In the end Annie agreed with me and threw them away.

Then there was this other time when she thought it might be fun to write jokey comments in library books, such as "Ho ho!" or "Ha ha!" or "Yuck!" I told her off about that one. I said it was vandalism and that I really, truly *hated* people that wrote things in books. *Or* turned down the corners of the pages. That is another thing I hate. I don't so much mind them doing graffiti in the school toilets as the school toilets are quite dim and dismal places and graffiti can sometimes make them brighter and more interesting. But books are precious! Well, they are to me. I know they are not to Annie, but after I'd lectured her she got quite ashamed and said that if I felt that strongly, she wouldn't do it. She does listen to me! Sometimes.

But she hardly listens to Rachel at all. She grumbled all the way downstairs.

"We don't *want* to go downstairs! There isn't anything to *do* downstairs. We want to stay in my bedroom. It's not fair! It's my house as much as yours! What right have you got to tell me where I can go in my own house?"

"Every right!" snarled Rachel. "I'm the one who's been left in charge!"

"You're not supposed to push us about. You're only here to protect us in case anyone breaks in."

"I'm here to make sure you behave yourself!" shouted Rachel.

"I was behaving myself!"

"You were going to use that computer. You were going to do things you're not supposed to do! You get down there." Rachel gave Annie and me a little shove along the hall. "And you stay there!"

"But there isn't anything to *do* down here!" wailed Annie.

"Oh, don't be so useless!" Rachel herded us into the kitchen. "Go out in the garden and get some exercise!"

Rachel is a great one for exercise. She is an exercise *freak*. She is for ever charging fiercely up and down the hockey field, billowing clouds of steam, or dashing madly to and fro across the netball court. She also goes to the sports club twice a week and swims and jogs and does things with weights. This is why she is so lean and *toned*. In other words, super-fit. She thinks Annie and I ought to be super-fit, too. She is going to join the police when she is older. I just hope she goes and joins them up in Birmingham, or Manchester, or somewhere. Anywhere, so long as it is miles away from here! Here being Stone Heath, which is near Salisbury, and very quiet and peaceful, which it most certainly would not be if Rachel started bashing about with a truncheon. She'd whack people over the head just for *breathing*.

"Go on! Get out there," she said, flinging open the back door. "Go and get some fresh air, for a change. You're like a couple of couch potatoes!"

I said, "What's couch potatoes?"

 "Human beings that sit around doing nothing all day, like vegetables. Look at you! Megan's like a stick of celery, and as for you" – she poked poor Annie in the stomach – "you're like a water melon!"

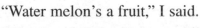

"Water melon's a fruit," I said.

"*Thank* you, Miss Know-it-All!"

"Don't you treat my friend like that," said Annie. "You've got no right to treat my friend like that, and just stop *shoving me*! Ow! Ouch! You're hurting!"

Rachel took absolutely no notice of Annie's howls; she is a really ruthless kind of person. She must have a heart like a block of cement. She drove me and Annie into the garden and for *over an hour* she made us throw balls at her so that she could whack them with a rounders bat. By the time she let us go back indoors we were completely exhausted.

"See what I mean?" she said. "You're so out of condition it's unbelievable! When I was your age I could run right round the playing field without even noticing it. You can't even run round the garden!"

She still wouldn't let us go back upstairs. She said *she* was going upstairs, and we were to stay in the sitting room until Mum came to collect me. Well! Quite honestly, we were so faint and wobbly from all the crashing about we'd done, chasing after the balls she'd whacked, we just sank down side by side on the sofa – a big shiny water melon and a little trembly stick of celery – and watched videos all afternoon. One of them was *Candyfloss*, which was the very first Harriet Chance I ever read! I know the film practically off by heart, word for word. If ever we did it as a school production, I could play the part of Candy, no problem! I would already know all my lines. Except that Candy has bright blue eyes "the colour of periwinkles", and blonde hair which "froths and bubbles", whereas I have brown eyes, more the colour of mud, I would say, and mousy *flat* hair, not a bubble in sight; so probably no one would ever cast me as Candy, more is the pity. But it doesn't really bother me; I wouldn't want to be an actor. I am going to be a writer, like Harriet!

RACHEL'S DIARY (THURSDAY)

I am just SO SICK of baby-sitting. Mum says, "For heaven's sake, Rachel! It's only a few weeks in the year." She also points out that I am being well paid for it, which is perfectly true. Mum and Dad pay me more than Jem gets paid for stacking shelves, AND I don't have to take fares out of it. Or food. But as I said to Mum, there is more to life than just money.

Mum pretended to be very surprised when I said this. Her eyebrows flew up and she went all sarcastic, saying, "Oh, really?" in this silly artificial voice. "Well, that's nice to know. You could certainly have fooled me!" A reference, I presume, to Christmas, when I was moaning — QUITE JUSTIFIABLY — about Gran giving me a box of bath salts. Bath salts, I ask you! *LAVENDER* bath salts. And a titchy little box, at that. Mum was quite cross. She reminded me that it was the thought that counted, to which I retorted that in Gran's case the thought obviously hadn't counted very much. Mum then told me not to be so grasping, but I don't see that it WAS grasping, considering Gran spends a small fortune going off on cruises every year, and that me and Annie are her only and dearly beloved grandchildren.

I mean, quite honestly, I wouldn't have minded so much if it had been something I wanted. But who in their right mind would pollute their bath water with stinky, flowery scents? Especially LAVENDER. Lavender's an old lady smell!

Anyway, that was then, and this is now. And right now I would rather be stacking shelves with Jem than stuck here in charge of a couple of horrible brats. Well, Annie is a horrible brat. She's plump, and she's spoilt! Her friend Megan isn't so bad, it's just that her mum is seriously weird, like some kind of pathetic old hen,

always fussing and bothering.
DON'T LET HER DO THIS,
DON'T LET HER DO THAT.
Plus she has this thing
about computers, like the
minute you log on someone's
going to leap out and grab
you. At least, thank goodness,
Mum and Dad have always been pretty relaxed about
trusting us to be sensible. I mean, how can you ever
LEARN to be sensible unless they let you just get on
with things? But Mum says if Mrs Hooper doesn't
want Megan going into chatrooms, then Annie has to
promise not to take her into chatrooms, and I have to
keep an eye on them both to make sure they're obeying
the rules. How am I supposed to do this? TIE THEM UP
AND HANDCUFF THEM??? Mum says don't be
ridiculous; just pop your head round the door every
now and then and check they're OK. But I don't see
why I should have to!

"Because it's what you're being paid for," says
Mum. "It's what I'd have to do, if I were here."

So why isn't she here? Because she wants to take
all of her holiday in one great lump and go off to

Spain for the summer. She seems to be under the impression that's what I want, too.

"Just think of those nice friends you made last year," she oozes.

Hm... I'm thinking of them. One in particular. The blond one. Kerry. He was gorgeous! But who's to say he'll be there again this year? In  any case, what about Ty? He's gorgeous, too! And he's stacking shelves in the supermarket... I might drop by there tomorrow. Jem says she and him are on the same shift. She says that sometimes they even stand and stock the same shelves together... I'm just glad she doesn't fancy him!!! Well, she does, but she's got Kieron. Otherwise I'd be tearing my hair out! I think tomorrow I'll definitely go down there. Just to suss things out. The two dwarfs can manage on their own for an hour or so. I mean, they're nearly twelve years old, for heaven's sake! That's quite old enough to start taking responsibility for themselves.

They're downstairs at the moment, watching a video. Moaning and whining because I made them go into the garden and run about. Left to themselves, they'd never move anywhere at more than snail's pace. The little fat thing is all squashy, like an overripe plum. The other one is so skinny she looks like a puff of wind would blow her over. They don't get enough exercise! If I had my way I'd make them do two laps of the hockey field every morning, before school. I think I'll get them running round the garden again tomorrow, before I go and see Jem. That way, they'll be too EXHAUSTED to get up to mischief.

Even if they're not, who cares? I'm sick to death of them!

two

MUM CAME TO collect me at four o'clock. Annie and me were still collapsed on the sofa, watching videos.

"You look as if you've had a busy day," said Mum.

I couldn't decide if that was her idea of a joke, or if she was being serious. Rachel was there. She said, "I made them go into the garden and get some exercise."

"Good for you!" said Mum.

"She only did it because she wanted to practise *hitting* things," said Annie.

"Excuse me," said Rachel, "I did it because you need to lose weight."

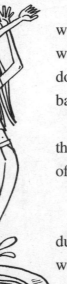

"Megan doesn't need to lose weight! If you've made her lose weight she'll probably disappear down the plughole next time she has a bath, and it'll be *all your fault*."

"I just hope they behaved themselves," said Mum. "It's very good of you, Rachel, to keep an eye on them."

"She's paid for it!" shrilled Annie.

"People are paid for emptying dustbins," said Mum, "but I wouldn't want to do it."

"It doesn't need any *skill*," said Annie. "You just have to be a big *bully*, is all."

Mum laughed. "Well! Sooner Rachel than me. I trust Megan hasn't been too much bother?"

"It's not Megan," said Rachel, looking hard at Annie. Annie stuck her tongue out. "It's *her*," said Rachel.

As Mum and me walked back through the Estate, Mum said that Annie was obviously "a bit of a handful".

Of course, I immediately leapt to the defence of my best friend.

"It's Rachel," I said. "She's so bossy!"

"It's difficult," said Mum, "when you're only sixteen. And after all, she has been left in charge."

I grumbled that it didn't give her the right to make us go and chase balls all round the garden.

"That's not what she's there for!"

"I'm sure she's doing her best," said Mum.

"*Bossy*," I muttered.

"Just keeping you out of trouble."

"We didn't need to be kept out of trouble! We weren't *in* trouble."

"Maybe she thought you were going to be."

"Well, we weren't!"

"You promise?"

"Promise!" I said. "We weren't *doing* anything."

"All right," said Mum. "I believe you."

Mum always does believe me, which is why I feel that I have to tell her the truth. It is quite hard at times!

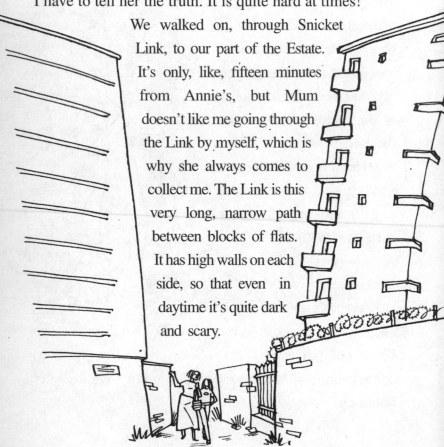

We walked on, through Snicket Link, to our part of the Estate. It's only, like, fifteen minutes from Annie's, but Mum doesn't like me going through the Link by myself, which is why she always comes to collect me. The Link is this very long, narrow path between blocks of flats. It has high walls on each side, so that even in daytime it's quite dark and scary.

Annie's mum doesn't seem to mind Annie going through it when she comes to visit me, but Mum says it's too dangerous. She says anyone could be lurking there. If I go to Annie's by myself I always take the long way round, by the road.

Annie lives in a house, but Mum and me live in a maisonette, which I know from French lessons means a *little* house. What it is, it's two little houses, one on top of the other. We have the one on top. It is quite tiny, but it is a real *little house*; not a flat!

Mum asked me what I was going to do after tea, and I said I was going to write my book review for school.

"Harriet Chance, I suppose?" said Mum. Mum knows all about Harriet Chance! She can hardly help it, considering my room is full to bursting with Harriet Chance books. "Which one are you doing?"

I said I was going to do *Candyfloss*, because a) I'd just watched the video – for about the ninety-eighth time! – and b) it was one of my favourites. This is what I wrote:

CANDYFLOSS

Candyfloss is eleven years old and lives with her mum. She has no brothers or sisters, but often wishes that she had. She has no dad, either. Her dad left home when Candy was only little, so that she can remember hardly anything about him. This makes her sad at times but mostly she is quite happy just to be with her mum.

I have just had a sudden thought: maybe this is why *Candyfloss* is one of my big favourites? Because Candy is like me! Lots of Harriet Chance characters are a bit like me, one way or another. For instance, there is Victoria Plum, who loves reading; and April Rose, who gets into trouble when her best friend leads her astray. But Candyfloss is the one who is *most* like me!

To continue.

Candy is quite a shy sort of person, who doesn't think very highly of herself. If anything happens, she always assumes she is in the wrong. Like if someone bumps into her in the street she will immediately say sorry, even if it was not her fault.

Like at school, just the other day, this big pushy girl called Madeleine Heffelump (that is what we  call her, her real name is Heffer) well, she came charging across the playground, straight towards me. I tried to get out of her way but I wasn't quick enough and she went crashing wham, bam, right into me, nearly knocking me over. And I was the one who said sorry. Just like Candy! Even though it was Madeleine Heffelump who was in the wrong, not me.

Crazy! Anyway. This is the rest of my review:

Candy is pretty, with bright blue eyes like periwinkles and bubbly blonde hair (as I already said, I don't look like her. Alas!) but she never thinks of herself as pretty, having this quite low opinion of herself most of the time. Then there is this girl at school, Tabitha Bigg, who bullies her and tells her she is useless and stupid, and Candy believes her, until one day a TV director comes to the school looking for someone to play a part in a TV show he is doing. Tabitha Bigg is sure he will choose her, because she is convinced she is the cat's whiskers and Utterly Irresistible. Candy is too shy to even show herself! She tries to hide in the lavatory, but she comes out too soon

and the director catches sight of her and immediately forgets all about Tabitha Bigg.

"THAT is the one I want!" he cries.

So Candy gets the part and it is yah boo and sucks to Tabitha Bigg, who is as sour as gooseberries and totally gutted. But everyone else is really glad that she didn't get chosen as they are all fed up with her.

When the show goes out on television, Candy's dad sees it (on the Net: he is in Australia) and he writes to Candy, and comes flying over to see her. It turns out that Candy's dad is a big name in Australian TV. He offers to take Candy back with him and make her a Big Star, but she chooses to stay with her mum.

Which is what I would do if ever my dad turned up! I wouldn't want to be a Big Star, and Candy doesn't, either. Another way that we are alike!

After I had written my review I read it out loud to Mum, who said that Candy sounded "a very sensible sort of girl".

I wondered if I was a sensible sort of girl, and whether sensible was an exciting thing to be. I decided that it wasn't, and that was why I needed Annie. I don't think anyone would call Annie sensible. But sometimes she is exciting. Like when she gets one of her mad ideas!

"When I go round there tomorrow," I said, "to Annie's, I mean, is it OK if I use her computer? Just to type out on?"

"What's wrong with your handwriting?" said Mum.

"It's horrible! No one can read it."

"Of course they can, if you just take care. Why don't you write it out again, nice and neatly? You can write beautifully when you try!"

I didn't want to try. I wanted to do it on Annie's computer! I wanted it to look like proper printing.

"Everyone else'll do it on the computer," I said.

"*Everyone?*" said Mum.

"Well... practically everyone."

"I don't believe you're the only person in your class who doesn't have their own PC."

"I said, *practically* everyone."

I think I must have looked a bit mutinous, a bit *rebellious*, 'cos Mum sighed and said, "Well, all right, if you really must. But I think it's a great shame if people are going to lose the ability to write by hand!"

"I don't mind for ordinary homework," I said, "but this is going to be made into a book. It's going to go on display. Miss Morton's going to put it in the library! So it needs to look *nice*, Mum. It—"

"Yes, yes, yes!" Mum held up her hands. "Enough! You've made your point."

"I wouldn't go into a chatroom," I said. "Honest! All I'm going to do is just type out the review. I wouldn't *ever* go into a chatroom," I said. "'cos we've talked about it. And I've given you my word. And I wouldn't ever break my word, Mum, I promise!"

"Oh, Megan." Mum reached out and patted my hand. "I know you think I'm a terrible old fusspot—"

"I don't, Mum," I said. "Truly!" I mean, I did, a bit; but I wanted her to know that I understood and that it didn't bother me.

"It's just that Annie is such a strong character—"

Did Mum mean that I was a weak one???

"—and you do tend to follow wherever she leads."

"Not always!" I said.

"Most of the time," said Mum.

"Only when it's something funny! I wouldn't do anything *bad*."

"I'm sure you wouldn't mean to. But it does worry me that Annie's parents are so lax."

I crinkled my forehead. "What does it mean? *Lax?*"

"They're not very strict with her. They let her do things that other parents wouldn't. Like going into chatrooms without supervision, or—"

"She knows not to give her address!" I said.

"Even so," said Mum. "She's only eleven years old. You can do very silly things when you're that age."

"Did you ever do silly things?" I said.

"Of course I did!" said Mum. "Everybody does. You don't have the experience to know any better."

"What were some of the silly things that you did?" I said.

"Oh, come on, Megs! You really don't want to hear about them."

"I do," I said. "I do!"

So then we got sidetracked, with Mum telling me how she'd once tried to turn herself blonde by using a bottle of household bleach – "I had to have all my hair cut off!" – and how another time she'd plucked her eyebrows almost raw, trying to look like some movie star I'd never heard of.

"Mum! To think you were so vain," I said.

"You'd be hard put to believe it now, wouldn't you?" said Mum, tweaking at the side of her hair where it is just starting to turn grey. "At least it's one thing I wouldn't accuse you of."

 It is true that on the whole I am not a vain sort of person, which is mainly because I don't really have anything to be vain about. Maybe if I was in a competition to find the human being that looks most like a stick of celery I might get a bit high and mighty, since I would almost certainly win first prize; or even, perhaps, a competition for the person with the most knobbly knees. My knees are *really* knobbly! A boy at school was once rude enough to say that my knees looked like big ball-bearings with twigs sticking out of them. Some cheek! But I have to admit he was right. So this is why I am not vain, as it would be rather pathetic if I was.

I told Mum about the celery competition and the ball-bearing knees, and Mum said, "Oh, sweetheart, don't worry! You'll fill out," as if she thought I needed comforting. But I don't! I don't mind looking like a stick of celery. I don't even mind knobbly knees! If ever I start to get a bit depressed or self-conscious, I just go and read one of my Harriet Chances. Every single one of Harriet's characters has secret worries about the way she looks. April Rose, for instance, has *no waist*. Me, neither! Victoria Plum has "hair like a limp dishcloth". Just like me! Then there is poor little Sugar Mouse, who agonises about

whether she will ever grow any boobs, and Fudge Cassidy, who can't stop eating chocolates and putting on weight.

I don't personally care overmuch about growing boobs, in fact I sometimes think I'd just as soon not bother with them. And as for putting on weight, Mum says I hardly eat enough to keep a flea alive (not true!) but there are lots of people who *do* agonise over these things. Harriet Chance knows everything there is to know about teenage anxieties. She can get right into your mind!

*

47

When Mum dropped me off at Annie's the next day, I said that I was allowed to use her computer just to type out my book review.

"We'd better tell *her*," said Annie. "Old Bossyboots."

"Oh, do what you like!" said Rachel, when Annie told her. "I've washed my hands of you."

"That's good," said Annie, as we scampered back to her bedroom. "P'raps now she'll leave us alone."

But she didn't. I'd just finished typing out my review when she came banging and hammering at the door, shouting to us "Get yourselves downstairs! Time for exercise!"

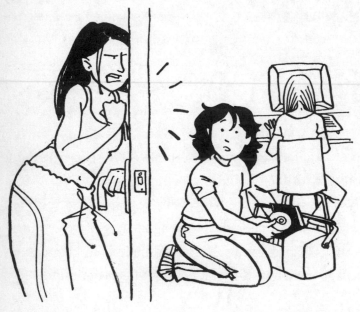

"We exercised yesterday," wailed Annie.

"So you can exercise again today!"

There wasn't any arguing with her.

"You get out there," she said. "It's good for you! You heard what your mother said, Megan."

She kept us at it until midday, by which time we had gone all quivering and jellified again.

"OK," she said. "That's enough! You can go back indoors now. I'm going out for a couple of hours. I want you to behave yourselves. *Otherwise*—" she twisted Annie's ear. Annie squawked.  "Otherwise, there'll be trouble. Geddit?"

"Goddit," said Annie. And, "Geddoff!" she bawled. "You're breaking my ear!"

"I'll do more than just break your ear," said Rachel, "if I get back and find you've been up to nonsense."

"She's not supposed to leave us on our own," said Annie, when Rachel had gone. "I'll tell Mum if she's not careful!" And then this big sly beam slid across her face, and she said, "This means we can do *whatever we want*, 'cos a) she won't find out and b) even if she does, there's nothing she can do about it! 'Cos if I tell Mum, Mum'll be furious with her. She promised your mum that Rachel would be here with us *all the time*."

"So what shall we do?" I said. "Watch more videos?"

"No! Let's get some lunch and take it upstairs."

"And then what?"

"Then we'll think," said Annie.

So we grabbed some food and went back to Annie's bedroom to eat it.

"Sure you don't want to visit the bookroom?" said Annie.

I said, "No! Don't keep pushing me."

"You don't know what you're missing," said Annie. "You'll never guess who I talked to!"

"Who?" I said.

"Harriet Chance's daughter!"

"*Lori?*"

"Mm!"

"You spoke to *Lori?*"

"Yes!"

I swallowed. "What did you talk about?"

Annie giggled and said, "You!"

"M-me?"

"I told her that you were Harriet's number-one fan. I told her you'd got every single book she'd ever written—"

"I haven't!" I cried. There are three of her early ones that I've only been able to find in the library, and one, called *Patsy Puffball*, that I have never even seen. (Though I did read somewhere that Harriet Chance was ashamed of it and wished she'd never written it.)

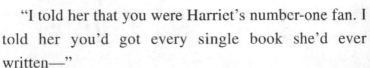

"I've got *most* of them," I said, "but I haven't got *all*."

"So what?" said Annie. "You're still her number-one fan! I thought you'd be *pleased* I'd talked about you!"

I suppose I should have been, but mainly what I was feeling at that moment was jealousy. Huge, raging, bright-green JEALOUSY. *I* was the bookworm! Not Annie. *I* was the one that ought to be talking to Harriet's daughter!

"We could visit right now," said Annie, "and see if she's there."

I pursed my lips and shook my head. Inside, I was seething and heaving like a volcano about to erupt.

"Megs, it's *harmless*!"

If I did erupt, I would spew bright-green vomit all over Annie. Great gobbets of it, splatting in her face and dripping through her hair.

"It's just *books*. Just people talking about *books*."

Annie didn't even like books. She only read them because of me.

"There's no grown ups. Nothing bad. No one talks about sex, or anything like that. It's just kids! Nobody over fourteen."

I came back to life. "If it's nobody over fourteen," I said, "what's Lori doing there?"

"Why?" Annie blinked, owlishly. "Is she over fourteen?"

"Yes, she is!" I knew all about Harriet Chance's daughter. I knew *everything there was to know* about Harriet Chance. Well, everything that had ever been written.

"So how old is she?"

"She's *fifteen*," I said. "She was fifteen in January."

"Oh! Wow! Fifteen!" Annie went into a mock fainting fit on the bed.

"You said nobody over *four*teen," I reminded her. "Anyone could just *say* they were fourteen!"

"Why would they want to? Just to talk about books!"

I hunched a shoulder. Annie had made me feel all cross and hot.

"OK, if you don't want to," she said. "I'll probably visit later and have a chat. I'll tell her you're too shy."

"Don't you dare!" I said.

"So what shall I tell her?"

"Tell her... tell her that I've chosen Harriet Chance as my favourite author and I'm writing a review of *Candyfloss* for the school library!"

"All right," said Annie. "I don't mind doing that."

Annie is a very generous and good-natured person. More good-natured than me, probably. She knew I was cross, but she didn't want to quarrel. Annie never quarrels. Rachel is the only person she ever gets ratty with; but then Rachel is enough to make a saint ratty, I would think.

"Hey!" Annie suddenly went bouncing off the bed. "Look what I've got!" She snatched up a box and rattled it at me.

"What is it?"

"Make-up! All Mum's old stuff that she doesn't want any more." Annie tipped the contents of the box on to her dressing table. Little tubs and pots rolled everywhere. "Loads of it!" she said. "Let's practise making ourselves up!"

So that was what we did. I still felt sore at the thought of Annie talking to Harriet Chance's daughter, but I was determined not to be tempted and I really didn't want to go on being cross, and messing about with the make-up was quite fun. After we'd made ourselves up to look beautiful — we thought! — we went a bit mad and started on Dracula make-up, and Cruella de Vil make-up. Alien-from-Outer-Space make-up. Monster-with-Red-Eyes make-up. Anything we could think of! We forgot all about Rachel. We were taken by surprise when she put her head round the door. She was taken by surprise, too.

"What on earth do you think you're doing?" she screeched.

Me and Annie flashed toothy lipsticky smiles at her. Annie had drawn black spider legs all round her eyes and daubed big red splotches on her cheeks. I had painted my mouth green and my eyes purple. In addition, we had both tied scarves round our chests, beneath our T-shirts, and stuffed them with knickers to give ourselves boobs. We could hardly look at each other without collapsing into giggles. It was really funny! Needless to say, Rachel didn't think so. She has *no* sense of humour. (She exercises too much. Well, that is my theory.)

"Honestly, you look a total sight," she said. "You'd better just scrub all that muck off yourself, Megan Hooper, before your mum comes for you!"

RACHEL'S DIARY (SATURDAY)

That tubby little scumbag has been whining to Mum about me making her exercise.

"M-u-u-u-um," she goes, "it's not fair! She hasn't any right!"

The really irritating thing is that Mum agrees with her. That is what is NOT FAIR. Mum always takes her side! She is so spoilt it is just not true. I was never spoilt like that.

Old Tubbo goes on wailing and moaning. "She made us run round the garden, Mum! She kept us out there for HOURS."

So Mum then tells me to "just let them be. Let them do their own thing."

I snap, "I thought I was supposed to be keeping an eye on them! How can I keep an eye on them if they're locked away upstairs?"

Mum says, "You wouldn't do anything naughty, would you, Annie? You know Megan's mum doesn't want her going into chatrooms?"

  To which Tub, all big-eyed and positively OOZING virtue, goes, "Mum, I KNOW. And I wouldn't, EVER. I wouldn't, Mum! HONESTLY."

And Mum believes her! Quite extraordinary. She never believed ME. She still doesn't. It always, like, the third degree when I've been anywhere.

"Are you SURE you didn't? Are you SURE you haven't? Are you telling me the truth?"

But with old Tub, it's like butter wouldn't melt in her mouth. She's such a sly boots! I wouldn't trust her further than I can spit.

"SEE?" She's all gloating and full of evil triumph. She doesn't actually say it out loud; she just mouths it at me. I mouth back at her. Something really rude, behind Mum's back. Fatso sticks her  tongue out. So childish! She then rushes across the room and twines herself round Mum, all cute and little-girly. Totally SQUIRM making.

"Tell her, Mum! Tell her she's not to boss us!"

"I'm sure she won't," says Mum, "so long as you behave yourselves."

"Mum, we do!"

Huh! is all I say to that. Huh huh HUH. But Mum accepts it. She says all right, that's all she wanted to hear. Later she gets me on my own and tells me to cool it.

"Give them a bit of leeway. They're not bad kids. You get on and do your thing, and let them do theirs." She then adds that, "You're not in the police force yet, you know!"

I tell her that it's the police SERVICE, not the police FORCE, which in fact I have already told her about two dozen times before, but Mum just waves a hand, like it's not important, and says, "Whatever! Go easy on them."

It's absolutely no use looking to Dad for support; he keeps well out of it. Bringing up girls is a woman's job. It's always "Ask your mum. See what your mum says." What a cop out! But then Dad is a bit of a throwback. Not a modern man at all.

Anyway, that has done it, as far as I am concerned. I wash my hands! They can stay upstairs and moulder all day long. What do I care if Little Goody Two-Shoes is led astray?

Besides, I have other things to think about. Well, one other thing, basically. TYRONE! Tyrone Patrick O'Malley. He's far more gorgeous than anyone I met on holiday. Mum can keep her Spanish boys! Jem says if it weren't for having Kieron, she would quite fancy him herself. But she has promised me faithfully not to do any ogling! I am still consumed with jealousy as they are still stacking shelves together.

Oh, I can't bear it! The thought of Jem actually standing next to him – maybe even TOUCHING him!!! It is agony. She says they're both on early shift next week, which means they finish at one, so if I go down there I can join them in the canteen for lunch. THEY get to eat free, but Jem says loads of people just drop in for a quick bowl of soup and a roll and butter. I can afford that! I could afford a whole three-course meal if it meant being with Ty!!!

The dear little girls will just have to get on by themselves. After all, it's only a couple of hours.

three

ON SUNDAYS ME and Mum always go off to visit my gran. It's a really long journey, as we have to catch a bus into town, then another bus out of town. It takes over two hours and is quite boring. Unfortunately, it is equally boring when we get there, as Gran's home where she lives is full of old ladies (and a few old men, though not very many) and there is absolutely nothing whatever to do. We can't even talk to Gran any more, as her mind has wandered and she doesn't know who we are. Sometimes she calls Mum "Molly", which we think was a friend of hers when she was young. Other times she calls her "Kathryn". We don't know who Kathryn was. She doesn't call me anything at all, which is sad, 'cos me and Gran were the hugest of friends when she lived with us.

In those days I didn't have to go round to Annie's in holiday time, as Gran was always there to look after me. We used to have such fun! We used to play board games, and word games, and read things to each other. Sometimes Annie would come and spend the day, and then we'd have even more fun! Gran used to laugh at Annie and the things she got up to. That was when she called her doolally.

"That girl is completely *doo*lally!"

I can't remember when Gran stopped laughing; when I was about ten, I think. Now she just sits there, staring. I don't really enjoy going to visit her. I don't mind so much about being bored, as I can always take a book to read, but it makes me unhappy to see Gran just sitting staring. And I *hate* that she doesn't know who I am! Mum says maybe she does know, somewhere deep inside. She says that is why we have to keep visiting.

"Imagine how hurt she'd be if there's a little part of her which can still recognise us, and we didn't come any more."

I couldn't bear for Gran to be hurt! Once or twice, when I've been really upset, Mum has said that perhaps she ought to leave me behind. Except that who could she leave me with?

"I can't keep parking you at Annie's."

Annie wouldn't mind; but when I think about what Mum said, that maybe there is a little part of Gran, somewhere deep down, that still recognises us, I know that I can't let Mum go by herself. I have to go with her; just in case.

To make myself a bit braver I always remember Clover in *Daisy and Clover*. Clover has to go and visit *her* gran in a home, and she feels just the same as I do. When Clover's gran doesn't know who she is, Clover says, "I wanted to burst into tears and cry, 'Gran, it's me! Don't you remember? All the things we used to do together?' But I didn't, because I knew it wouldn't be any use. Gran had gone, and there was no way of reaching her."

It is truly amazing how Harriet Chance describes every single thing I have ever felt or thought. Surely she must have been through it all herself? Or maybe she just has this incredible understanding of how it is to be a young person.

Some of the old ladies in Gran's home are what Mum calls "real characters". (What Gran would probably have called *doo*lally.) There is one who is a particular friend of mine. Her name is Mrs Laski, but I call her Birdy as she is very tiny and fragile, and she speaks in this high twittery voice, like a bird. Me and Birdy have these long, interesting conversations together. Like Birdy might say, "It's very whizzbang out there today." That is one of her expressions: *whizzbang*. I don't quite know what it means, but lots of things are whizzbang.

"Whizzbangs all over the place! They're arriving in hordes! Did you find any?"

And I will cry, "Yes! I found loads!"

She likes it when I play the game the way she wants it played. She does *not* like it if I am stupid enough to say something such as, "Found any what?" That makes her cross. But so long as I answer *intelligently*, we can go on for ages! Birdy will ask me what colour they were, these things that I had found loads of. I will say, "Red! Bright red!" Then Birdy will say, "Not green?" – I mean, this is just an example – and I will say, "Well, maybe some of them were," and she will nod and say, "I thought so! It's the time the of year. Very whizzbang! They're all on their way. Swarms of them!" And before I know it we will be in outer

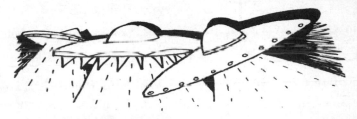

space, surrounded by aliens, all whizzbanging about in their flying saucers, on their way to earth to suck out our brains. Everything always comes back to the aliens sucking out our brains.

Harriet Chance has never written about anyone like Birdy. Maybe I should write and suggest it to her! Except that I once read she almost never uses ideas that come from other people. She says she has "a resistance" to them.

There is another old lady in Gran's home whose name I don't know so I call her Mrs Yo-Yo, because her favourite toy is a yo-yo. She yo-yo's away like crazy! I know it is very sad, when maybe she has been something important in life, and had a job and brought up children,

and now she does nothing but play with a yo-yo all day, but at least she is happy. She beams, and laughs, and skips. I would rather Gran played with a yo-yo than just sat in a chair doing nothing.

Mrs Yo-Yo wasn't there that Sunday, but Birdy was. We had a bit of a chat about whizzbang dustbins full of aliens come to suck our brains out, then a woman that I think is her daughter came and took her away. She said, "She's not on about aliens again, is she?"

I said, "Yes, they're hiding in the dustbins," and the woman looked embarrassed and said she was so sorry and that I wasn't to take any notice. I don't know what she said she was sorry for! I enjoy my conversations with Birdy. She has a really good imagination.

After she had gone, and Mum was sitting with Gran, telling her all the things that had been going on in our lives during the week (which was not a lot. Nothing as interesting as aliens hiding in dustbins) I settled down to finish my project for school. I'd done the review; now I had to do the biography. Biography of Harriet!

I'd looked her up on the Internet at school, and I'd also read about her in a book called *Children's Writers*. Plus, of course, the little bits that publishers put at the front of books, like telling you where the author lives and how many children they've got. Plus an interview that she had done for a magazine which is in the school library. I knew everything there was to know! I could have written a whole book about Harriet. But our teacher had said not more than three hundred words, so I thought it would give me good practice in picking out the things which were most important. Otherwise I would just go on for ever! Annie had asked what was the *least* number of words, as she didn't think she'd be able to manage more than about twenty. Other people were just going to copy out stuff they'd read. I don't think there is any fun in that.

I settled myself at a little table in the corner and turned back the cover of my nice new writing block.

69

BIOGRAPHY OF HARRIET CHANCE

Harriet Chance was born in Epsom, Surrey, on 12th March 1962. She went to school at the Convent of the Sacred Heart. She was very good at English, French and German, and very bad at maths and geography. She hated playing hockey. (Just like me!)

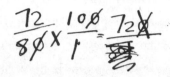

$$\frac{72}{80} \times \frac{100}{1} = \frac{72}{1}$$

When she left school she went to university in London and did English. After that she went to teach at a school in Birmingham, where she met her husband and got married. She now lives in London with her husband and her daughter Lori, who is fifteen.

Harriet Chance started writing books while she was at school. When she was twelve she wrote a book called PAPER DOLLS, but she never tried to get it published. When she was at university she wrote some poetry which was not very good. While she was a teacher she wrote a book for grown-ups, but that was not very good either so for a while she gave up writing.

Then she got married and had a baby and didn't work any more but she got bored just being at home all the time and so she started writing again.

Her very first book that was published was called PATSY PUFFBALL, but now she wishes she had never written it. She would like all the copies to be put into a shredding machine. She really hates that book!

Other books she has written include: CANDYFLOSS, VICTORIA PLUM, APRIL ROSE, SUGAR MOUSE and FUDGE CASSIDY. In all she has written fifty-four. Her latest one is called SCARLET FEATHER. It is about this girl called Scarlet whose mum and dad split up and Scarlet has to decide which one she will live with. I cannot say which one she chooses as the book is not yet published. But I can say that Harriet Chance

is my ACE FAVOURITE AUTHOR!

~~~~~

I had just written the last words and put a little squiggly bit underneath to show that that was The End, when an old lady I had never seen before suddenly spoke to me.

"And what are *you* writing?" she said. "Love letters?"

My cheeks immediately went bright pink. (I don't know why, but I am very easily embarrassed.) I said, "No, I'm doing a project for school."

"What is it about? Is it about love?"

I shook my head, turning even pinker.

"Is it about *boys*?"

"N-no," I said. "It's about my f-favourite author."

"Does she write about *love*?"

I shook my head again; more vehemently, this time.

"So what does she write about?"

"J-just... ordinary p-people," I said. "And their p-problems."

"Ah. An agony aunt! I used to read Enid Blyton. Do you read Enid Blyton?"

I said, "S-sometimes."

"I used to read her *all* the time. Which ones have you read?"

"Um... *F-Five on a T-Treasure Island*?"

"Ah, yes! The Famous Five. What else?"

"N-Noddy?"

"Noddy? I should have thought you were rather too old for Noddy."

"When I was l-little," I said.

"Oh, my dear," said this strange old woman, "you are still little! But too old for Noddy. Try *The Secret Island*. That was one of my favourites!"

With this she wandered off, and I was quite relieved. I didn't mind talking to Birdy about aliens, but I don't like the sort of conversations that make my cheeks go pink. It may be *silly* that they turn pink, but there is nothing that I can do about it. It is just something that happens.

I watched the old lady shuffle across the room. I wondered how old she was. I thought probably about eighty. I mean, she was *really* old. Older than Gran, even though Gran sat staring and this old lady could still walk and talk. To think that she was reading Enid Blyton over sixty years ago! Over *seventy* years ago. I tried to imagine how it might be when I was her age, tottering about in an old people's home, asking young girls who had come to visit their grans if they had ever read Harriet Chance. I couldn't! I just couldn't  *imagine* being eighty years old. But I could imagine people still reading Harriet Chance. I bet they'll still be reading her in a hundred years' time!

"What was that all about?" said Mum, as we walked up the road to catch our bus back to town.

"She wanted to know what I was writing," I said.

"And what were you writing?"

"My biography of Harriet!"

"Oh, yes... didn't you say something about a new book being published?"

"*Scarlet Feather*," I said; and I sighed.

"What's the sigh for?" said Mum.

"It's in hardback... it won't be out in paperback for *ages*."

"Well, who knows?" said Mum. She patted her bag. "Gran's just given me your birthday present... so maybe you'll be able to buy it?"

Gran doesn't really give me birthday presents any more. It's Mum who buys the book tokens and then guides Gran's hand as she signs the birthday card. But we both pretend. I always give Gran a big kiss and say thank you. Maybe somewhere deep inside she knows what it's for.

The phone was ringing as we got back home. It was Annie, all bright and bubbling. She is always bright and bubbling.

"Hey! Guess what?" she went. "I think I know what your birthday prezzie's going to be!"

I said, "What? What?"

"Can't tell you! I'm still arranging it. But it's something you're absolutely going to *love*."

I went, "Hm!" thinking that if it was anything gluey I wouldn't use it. I didn't care how much it hurt Annie's feelings. I didn't want my eyes swelling up again! I looked like a football that'd been kicked by David Beckham.

"I've been speaking to you-know-who," said Annie.

I squeaked, "*Lori?* You've been speaking to Lori again?"

"For ages!"

Now I'd gone all green and jealous.

"What did you speak about?"

"'Bout you."

"About *me*? What did you say?"

"Tell you tomorrow! It's so exciting!"

"What? What is?"

"What we've been speaking about!"

"*Annieeeee!* Tell me!"

But she wouldn't. She just giggled, and bounced the phone back down. I went into the kitchen and said, "Mum, I'm so envious! I can't help it."

"Envious of what?" said Mum.

"Envious of Annie! She's been talking—" I took a breath "—to *Harriet Chance's daughter*!"

"Oh, my goodness," said Mum. "Where did she meet her?"

"In a bookroom. On the Internet." I could already see the frown lines gathering on Mum's forehead.

Hastily, I gabbled on. "It's this special site, just for bookworms. That's what it's called... *Bookworms*."

"I see." Mum smiled. The frown lines had disappeared. Hooray! "Now, I suppose, you're just dying to get on there and talk to her yourself?"

"Couldn't I, Mum? Just this once? It's not a chatroom! It's *educational*. All about books. It would be just *sooo* useful, for my project!"

"I'll tell you what," said Mum. "I'll make you a promise... birthday treat! Next weekend we'll ask Annie's mum if we can both call round and you can use Annie's computer and go and have a little chat. On your birthday! How about that?"

Of course I said that it would be lovely; I didn't want to sound ungrateful. But somehow I just couldn't manage to feel enthusiastic. It was something to do with the fact that Mum would be there, and that it was all being planned in advance. Annie didn't have to plan in advance! She just logged on, and started chatting. She didn't have her mum looking over her shoulder to check what she was talking about. If I talked to Harriet's daughter, I wanted it to be strictly confidential! Just the two of us. Otherwise I'd get embarrassed. There'd be things I couldn't say, if I thought Mum was watching.

"Tell Annie, tomorrow," said Mum. "I'll have a word with her mum. I'm sure it'll be all right... Bookworms in the morning, party in the afternoon. Never say I don't indulge you!"

RACHEL'S DIARY (SUNDAY)

That Annie! She's up to something, I know she is. The phone rang this evening and I went to answer it and it was Mrs Hooper, wanting to speak Mum. I thought she was ringing to complain about me making them take a bit of exercise. Either that, or she'd discovered that old Tubby Scumbag had gone and got her dear little angel to visit a site with her, which would never surprise me. She is certainly up to SOMETHING.

So, anyway, I braced myself for trouble, thinking either way I'd be the one to get the blame, I mean I always am. Leastways, that's how it seems to me. Of course I may just have a persecution complex, but I doubt it. I don't IMAGINE these things. Well, but hooray! This time it wasn't anything to do with me.

Wonders will never cease. For once in my life, I haven't done anything wrong.

All it was, was the little angel's mum wanting to know if the little angel could come round on Saturday and play with the computer. UNDER SUPERVISION. Natch! Mum said, "I told her that would be all right. It seems there's some special chatroom she wants to visit... something to do with books?"

"Bookworms," said the Scumbag.

"Well, that sounds harmless enough. But her mum wants to be there with her."

"Really?" said Dad.

"She's read all these scare stories... people pretending to be what they're not."

The Scumbag said that didn't happen in the bookroom. "Everyone just talks about books. *Children's* books. Grown-ups don't read children's books."

I said, "So what?"

"So they wouldn't be able to talk about them," said my little clever clogs sister. I pointed out that they might be able to talk about Harry Potter, everyone can talk about Harry Potter, but she said Megan wouldn't want to.

"She's not into Harry Potter. She'd want to talk about H.C."

Mum said, "Who's H.C.?" but at this the Scumbag went all silly and dissolved into giggles.

"I can understand her worries," said Mum (referring, I suppose, to Mrs Hooper). "Megan's her only child, and it can't be easy, bringing a child up on your own... but I do think she keeps her a bit too wrapped up in cotton wool."

"Or maybe we're being a bit complacent?" suggested Dad.

"But they've got to learn," said Mum. "How are they going to learn if they're never allowed to take any responsibility? We've already been through this, haven't we, Annie?"

"Yes," said the Scumbag, with a big saintly beam.

"You never give your address to anyone, do you?"

"No way!" said the Scumbag, beaming brighter than ever.

"Or your telephone number?"

"Mum, I wouldn't!"

"You see? Annie KNOWS," said Mum. "Poor little Megan's still a total innocent. She could never be left on her own, she'd get into all sorts of trouble. Anyway, they're coming round Saturday morning, then you're off to her party in the afternoon. Have you got her a present yet?"

"Working on it," said the Scumbag.

"Well, don't leave it too late. What are you going to buy?"

The Scumbag said she wasn't going to BUY anything.

"You mean you're making something?" said Mum. "That's nice!"

So then the Scumbag giggled again, for absolutely no reason whatever as far as I could see. That is what makes me suspicious. She is being all secretive and over-excited about something. I notice these things! With Mum and Dad, it's like they're wearing blindfolds.

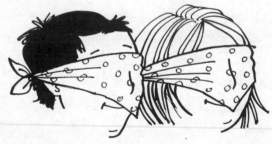

Another thing that makes me suspicious. A few minutes ago I angrily hammered on her bedroom door demanding to know what she'd done with my heated rollers that she keeps snitching. She actually APOLOGISED. Which come to think of it is quite suspicious in itself. The Scumbag saying sorry!!!

"I forgot," she said. "I put them in my cupboard."

While she was getting them out of the cupboard (but what cheek to put them in there in the first place!) I happened to glance down at some drawing she was doing.

"What's this?" I said. "Is this Megan's birthday present?"

"It's her birthday card."

"Weird kind of card," I said. She'd drawn this picture of a sticklike child on her knees, and a woman wearing a halo round her head, with a speech bubble coming out of her mouth saying, HAPPY BIRTHDAY! "What's it meant to be?"

By way of reply, the Scumbag picked up a felt tip pen and wrote H.C. in big bold letters with an arrow pointing to the woman.

"Who is H.C.?"

She wouldn't tell me. All she did was giggle again. Definitely something going on! But I have washed my hands. It's the parents' job to know what their children are up to.

four

I COULD HARDLY wait to get round to Annie's the next day! I was, like, jigging up and down with impatience all the time Mum was getting ready. Usually in the mornings she just grabs her bag and that's that, we're off! Today, wouldn't you know it, she suddenly decides her shoes are killing her and she's got to change into different ones. Then while she's changing her shoes she notices this *teeny little hole* in her tights, and instead of sticking it up with nail varnish, which is what she'd normally do, she has to take the tights off and find herself a new pair.

I felt like screaming, "Mum! Who's going to see them?" I mean, she works in an office, sitting at a desk. No one's going to notice holes in her tights! Specially not ones you'd need a *magnifying glass* to find. But Mum likes to keep herself looking nice. She's always very neat. Unlike Annie's mum, who looks like a haystack! A very soft, comfortable sort of haystack; but still a haystack.

"What's the matter?" said Mum, as I stood in her bedroom doorway, wrapping one leg round the other. "Do you want to go to the toilet?"

I said, "*Muuum!*"

"Well, what are you jigging about for?"

"It's late," I said. "You'll be late for work!"

Mum's never late for work; she's a very punctual sort of person. "It's nearly half-past nine," I said.

"That's all right," said Mum. "I don't have to be in till ten... stocktaking on Thursday, right? Late night. So I get a ten o'clock start the rest of the week! What's your rush, anyway?"

"Got things to do," I said.

"Oh! I suppose you want to talk to Annie about Saturday?" Mum laughed. "Come on, then! Let's get you over there."

I did feel a bit mean, not being more enthusiastic about Mum's idea of letting me visit the bookroom. I knew it was a big thing for her. She is not scared of technology as she uses a computer for work; but she definitely gets twitchy when I want to do some of the things that anyone else's mum would let them do without even winking an eyelash. Or is it batting an eyelid? (But how could you *bat* an eyelid? It would hurt!) I knew she'd spoken to Annie's mum and Annie's mum had said it would be OK, and I was quite looking forward to it;

but mostly I wanted to hear what Annie had been saying to Lori. What had she been telling her about me???

When we arrived at Sylvan Close, which is the road where Annie lives, Annie's mum and dad had already left for work and Annie was in the middle of a big shouting match with Rachel. You could hear them going at it as you went up the path.

"This sounds serious," said Mum. "Is it safe to go off and leave them?"

"It's OK," I said, "they're always having rows. They don't *do* anything. They just yell."

It was all about heated rollers, which Rachel said Annie had taken, and Annie swore she'd given back.

"I gave them back *last night*!"

"So where are they, then?"

"How should I know? You took them!"

"I beg your pardon, *you* were the one that took them!"

Rachel then shouted that she was sick of Annie just helping herself to things that didn't belong to her and if there was any more of it she was going to put a padlock on her bedroom door. "Because you're a thieving little toerag!"

Phew. I am sometimes quite glad that I am an only child.

"Can we go upstairs now?" I said.

"You can do whatever you like!" snapped Rachel. "I've washed my hands of you!"

With that she stalked off in a huff and Annie and me went up to Annie's bedroom.

"Good riddance!" yelled Annie, as somewhere downstairs a door slammed shut. "I gave her back her stupid rollers! How should I know what she's gone and done with them? W—"

"Oh, look, just shut up!" I begged. "I want to hear what you talked to Lori about!"

"Yes. Well!" Annie hurled herself down on to her bed. "I was telling her all about you, right? About you being a big fan, and everything. How you were doing this project for school. How you had all these books, and—"

"Yes, yes, you told her that before!" I said.

"So, OK, I told her again. I wanted her to know that you were this huge great admirer, and I said how it was your birthday on Saturday and how you really, really wanted this new book, this Feather thing—"

"*Scarlet Feather!*"

"*Scarlet Feather*, and—"

"You weren't trying to get her to send me one?" I said, horrified.

"Why not? I thought you wanted one!"

"I do, but not like that! That's like *begging*."

"Well, it's all right," said Annie, "'cos she didn't offer anyway. I thought she might have, 'cos I bet when books are published the authors get given loads of free copies,

I mean like stacks and stacks, so it wouldn't have hurt, but—"

"It would've hurt me!" I said.

Annie looked at me and shook her head. "You're weird," she said. "You know that? You're really weird!"

"Now she probably won't ever want to talk to me!" I wailed. "She'll think you were just trying to get a book out of her!"

"No, she won't," said Annie. "I've got it all arranged."

"Got what all arranged?"

Annie bounced upright, on the bed. She hugged her knees to her chest and grinned this big triumphant grin, almost splitting her face in two. "Your birthday present. I'm arranging it. *Lori's* arranging it. With her mum."

"With Harriet?"

Annie nodded, happily. "She's really nice! Really friendly. Not a bit stuck up. She asked me if you'd ever met her mum, and I said no, but you would absolutely love to. I said if you could meet her it would be the most exciting thing that had ever happened to you – 'cos it would, wouldn't it?" said Annie.

I gulped. "Yes, it would!"

"So Lori said, being as you're such a huge great fan and you're doing this project and everything, she'd ask her mum if it could be arranged. She's almost sure her mum'll say yes. So there you are!"

Annie flung her legs in the air and exultantly rolled backwards on the bed. "You're going to meet Harriet Chance!"

"B-but... h-how?" I said.

"What d'you mean, how?"

"Well, I mean... she's in London!"

"No, she's not."

"She used to be."

"So people move! We can get to her easy as anything on the bus. I didn't give her your *address*," said Annie, "'cos I know you're not supposed to—"

"She's got it anyway," I said. "I mean, Harriet has." When I was ten I wrote her this creepy crawly fan letter, all decorated with hearts and flowers, and she wrote back, saying *Love from Harriet, XXX,* and I was so thrilled! I put the letter in a special frame and hung it on the wall. It's still there, even now.

"Yes, well, this is it," said Annie. "I probably *would* have given it to her if she'd offered to send you a book, but all she did was just ask what part of the country we lived, and when I said Wiltshire she said was it anywhere near Salisbury, so I said yes, and she said in that case there was no problem. She's going to ask her mum and see when to do it. It will be your birthday treat," said Annie, all self-important. "A special present from me to you! You might try to look a bit *happy* about it."

I said, "I am happy! It would be the most brilliant birthday present I've ever had!"

"So why are you looking worried?"

"I'm just scared in case it doesn't happen!"

"It will happen. Lori's promised."

"But why should someone important like Harriet want to see *me*?"

"Because you're her number-one fan! Because you're doing this thing about her! Because it's your *birthday*. I told you I was going to give you a really good present! You didn't believe me, did you? You thought I was going to give you something stupid, like last year."

I bleated a protest. "I didn't!" The reason I bleated was that I was in such a tremor my voice had gone. I'd swallowed my voice! "I didn't," I said, "honestly!"

"Bet you did," said Annie.

"I did *not*. You always give me good presents!"

"Not as good as this. I'm your fairy godmother!" Annie sprang off the bed and did a little twirl. "I'm the one that makes your dreams come true!"

I thought that meeting Harriet really would be a dream come true. I'd read once where she'd visited a school to talk about her books, and I had just been *so jealous* of the people at that school. Annie couldn't understand, as her dream would be to meet someone from her favourite band, which at that moment was Dead Freaks.

I thought Dead Freaks were really creepy! But Annie had all their albums, just like I have all of Harriet's books, so sometimes I would listen to Dead Freaks and sometimes Annie would read Harriet Chance. That is what friendship is all about, sharing each other's interests even if you don't really understand them.

"When do you think we'll know?" I said.

"Soon as Lori's spoken to Harriet. Tomorrow, maybe? I said it would be best if it was in the afternoon, 'cos then we could go while old Bossyboots is out, so she wouldn't be able to stop us."

"How d'you know she'll be out?"

"'Cos she's got this thing about one of the boys in Savemore. Ty*rone*." Annie pulled a face. "He's really gross!

96

But she's got the hots for him. So she has to keep going there every day to check her friend Jem hasn't pinched him. See, they're stacking shelves and she's stuck here babysitting, which is why she's in such a tetch. But it means we can go and meet Harriet and she won't know anything about it! Well, not until we get back, and she won't be able to say anything 'cos she's not meant to leave us on our own. And I don't think, probably, that we ought to say anything, either. Not even to your mum, 'cos I know what you're like."

I said, "What am I like?"

"You tell her everything," said Annie.

"I don't tell her *everything*." I'd never told her about hiding in the stationery cupboard. I'd never told her about the birds' nests.

"Well, you'd better not tell her about this," said Annie. "Not unless you want her coming with us! She's already going to listen in on Saturday. You don't want her sitting there while you talk to Harriet, do you?"

I had to admit, I didn't. I definitely didn't! If I was going to meet Harriet I wanted it to be *private*. Just the two of us. Well, and Annie, of course. But I didn't mind Annie. She's my best friend and we don't have any secrets. But it would be really offputting if Mum was there!

"Let's listen to music," said Annie; and she snatched up this one CD that is my least, *least* favourite of Dead Freaks as it is quite scary, well I think it is, but Annie just loves it. She doesn't usually play it when I am around, but this time she said that I "owed her", and I couldn't deny it, so we were sitting there listening when the door crashed open and it was Rachel, shouting at us to "Turn that music down! They'll complain next door, and I'll be the one that gets into trouble!" She then added that she was going out and would be back in a couple of hours and we were to just behave ourselves *or else*.

"Else what?" said Annie.

"Else you'll be in deep ****!"

The reason I have put **** is so as not to write what she actually said, as what she actually said was quite rude and I don't think really she ought to have said it; but as she was in this strop on account of having to baby-sit for me and Annie instead of stacking shelves with Ty*rone*, I forgave her. The minute she'd gone, Annie turned the music up again.

"Now we can have *fun*!" she said.

I was in a state of jitters again next morning, desperate to get round to Annie's and discover if she'd managed to speak to Lori again, but I did my best to contain myself as I didn't want Mum growing suspicious, thinking I was up to something. The minute she dropped me off, we raced upstairs to Annie's bedroom. I could see that Annie was bursting with news.

I said, "Well? Did you speak to her?"

Annie's face broke into a big beam. "Yes! It's all arranged. We're going to have tea with her!"

I said, "*Tea*..." I could hear my voice, all hushed and breathy, like it was going to be tea with the Queen.

Only this was far more exciting! I wouldn't have anything very much to say to the Queen. I'd got simply loads to say to Harriet!

"We're going on Thursday," said Annie. "I thought Friday would have been better, 'cos of being nearer to your birthday, but Lori said her mum couldn't manage Friday. And I said we couldn't manage Saturday 'cos of your birthday party, so she said what about Thursday, and I said Thursday would be OK, so—"

"Thursday is good!" I said. "Mum has to work late on Thursday!"

"Anyway, we'll be back ages before then," said Annie. "It's only *tea*. What we've got to do, she said, is get a bus to Brafferton Bridge—"

"We go through there on the way to visit Gran!" I knew exactly which bus, and where to catch it: a number six, at the back of Market Square. "Is Brafferton Bridge where she lives?" I said, thinking that I would have to change the first bit of my biography.

"Near Brafferton Bridge. She said her mum will meet us and take us back. Lori won't be able to come 'cos she's already doing something else, but—"

"That's all right."

I didn't care about Lori; Harriet was the one I cared

about. In fact I thought I might be a bit shy if Lori were there, so I was quite glad she wasn't going to be.

"She said maybe we could meet another time," said Annie. "She sounds really nice! Oh, and it's got to be kept a secret. She said her mum doesn't usually meet her fans 'cos if she met all the people that read her books she'd never have time for writing."

"Yes." I nodded. I'd read that somewhere, in one of the interviews that Harriet had given. She had said that she was a very private person. She loved to hear from her readers, and she always, *always* wrote back; but she didn't very often make public appearances. I could understand that! That is probably how I would be, if I were a famous writer.

"So we've not got to tell *anybody*," said Annie. "In case it gets back to people and they all want to come."

"Absolutely!" I said. This was *my* treat. I could think of several girls in our class who would be really envious... but I certainly didn't want them intruding on my birthday present!

"I said what we'd do," said Annie, "we'd look up the times of buses so I could tell Lori which one we were getting so Harriet doesn't have to be kept waiting."

I was ever so impressed! Annie isn't normally what I would call an efficient sort of person. Mrs Glover at school once told her she was "slapdash". But because this was my birthday present, and she did so much want me to enjoy it, she was making this huge great effort. She even knew how to look up bus timetables on the Internet!

"See, look? There's one that gets to Brafferton Bridge at ten past two. I'll tell her that one. Then you talk as much as you like, all about books, you could even do an interview, then we can have tea and come back home and nobody will ever know! Now you're looking worried again. What's the matter *now*?"

"How are we going to recognise her?" I said.

"Who, Harriet?"

"There aren't any photos!"

I'd searched and searched, but being such a private person she obviously didn't like having her photograph taken. (I agree! I don't, either.) All these other old ugly authors had their pictures all over the place – well, they weren't all old and ugly, but they weren't very beautiful, either, which I suppose oughtn't to matter as it is their books you are interested in, and not their faces, and even if Harriet turned out to be old and ugly I would still be her number one fan! But the only photographs I had been able to find were taken when she was young. I knew it was when she was young as she was holding Lori, and Lori was just a baby. Harriet had looked really pretty, then, with a nice little round squashy face and dark hair, with a fringe. I did hope she still looked like that! But I knew it was a long time ago, almost fifteen years. People could change a whole lot in fifteen years. I mean, anyone who had last seen me when I was, say, *two*, certainly wouldn't recognise me as I am now. So I thought probably she was bound to look a little bit different.

"We don't want to get in a car with the wrong person!" I said.

Annie rolled her eyes. "You are such a worrygut! Maybe she could hold a copy of one of her books? Or d'you think there might be hundreds of people waiting at Brafferton Bridge holding copies of books?"

I giggled at that.

"I'll ask Lori," said Annie. "Just leave it to me. And *stop FUSSING*!"

RACHEL'S DIARY (THURSDAY)

My sister is a brat. An obnoxious, odious, beastly
little BRAT. She was playing music really loud this
morning. So loud the floors were practically shaking.
I told her to turn it down, but the minute I left the
house she went and turned it back up again. I could
hear it thumping and banging all the way down the
road. Next Door's going to create, I just know they
are. Then Mum'll say, "Rachel, how could you let her
annoy the neighbours like that? You KNOW what Mrs
Hawthorn's like about noise!" And it
will stand there looking all
simpering and saintly, and
pulling faces at me behind
Mum's back. It knows I can't say
anything. If I complain about
it not doing what it's told,
it'll go and tell Mum about

me going off to meet Ty instead of staying here and playing nursemaid. It's blackmail!

Well, and what do I care? Seeing Ty is the only thing I care about. He's asked me to go to a party with him on Saturday!!! I bet he never would have if it weren't for me going in every day and sitting there right under his nose. He probably wouldn't ever have noticed me! You have to work at these things, they don't happen by themselves. Well, sometimes they do, if you're lucky, but mostly I think you have to make a bit of an effort, specially if it's someone like Ty that could have the pick of the bunch. He's so gorgeous! He used to go out with Marsha Williams, but he doesn't any more so it's not like I'm stealing him. He was up for grabs! I wouldn't have made a play for him if he'd still been going with Marsha. At least, I don't think I would. But then again, I might have! All's fair in love and war, and Marsha is a total dimbo anyway. She may have the boobs but she certainly hasn't got the brains. She doesn't deserve a boy like Ty.

The brat and its friend are downstairs now, hatching plots. I know they're hatching plots because whenever I come into the room they immediately stop talking and look guilty. MEGAN looks guilty. Annie looks furtive. When I ask what's going on, Megan turns bright pink and Annie says, "Nothing. Why?" I say, "Because your eyes have suddenly bunched up and gone all shifty." So then she crosses her eyes and sticks out her tongue, and I tell her she ought to have a bit more respect for those in authority — i.e. me — to which she retorts that I am not in the police force YET. I snap, "Service!" and flounce from the room; whereupon they both start giggling.

They just don't seem to teach kids any manners these days. I'm sure when I was that age I wouldn't have cheeked my older sister like Annie cheeks me. If I'd had an older sister. If I had, I'd have paid attention and done what she told me. I would have taken the opportunity to LEARN. This one just doesn't care. Well, and neither do I! Let them get on with it.

five

THURSDAY CAME – THE day of my birthday treat! I was so excited, but a bit nervous, as well. I had been Harriet's number-one fan for so long! Ever since I was eight years old, and read *Candyfloss*. I just loved that book! I read it so many times that in the end it fell to pieces and Mum had to buy me another one. Now I was actually going to meet the person who had written it!

I couldn't make up my mind what to wear. I don't have all that many clothes in my wardrobe, and I am not one of those hugely fashion-conscious people, like this girl at school, Rozalie Dunkin, who is trendy as can be and always dressed in the latest gear, which Mum won't let me have. Or at least, not very often. She either says it's cheap and tacky, or she says it's not suitable. Meaning that she doesn't approve of eleven-year-olds dressing up like they're eighteen. She really is very old-fashioned, my mum. It doesn't usually bother me as I don't specially want to go round pretending to be eighteen, and am probably a little bit old-fashioned myself. Annie sometimes says I am. But I did want to look nice for Harriet!

I dithered for ages, trying to decide. Most of the stuff in my wardrobe is stuff that Rozalie Dunkin wouldn't be seen dead in. But I had to wear something! Mum was calling to me from the kitchen: "Megan, your breakfast is ready! What are you doing?"

I stuck my head out of the door and yelled, "Getting dressed!"

"Well, just be quick! I haven't got all day."

Now it was Mum agitating to go, and me holding things up. I stopped dithering, grabbed a top which was not new but which I just happen to love – it is blue, with little bunched sleeves, and ties round the middle – and my best pair of jeans, which *were* new. So new I hadn't yet worn them! They had beautiful embroidered bits round the bottom, bright reds and greens, all curling and swirling. I thought maybe they were the one thing I owned that Rozalie Dunkin might not mind being seen dead in. I didn't have any trendy sort of shoes, so I just put on my trainers, which she definitely would *not* have been seen dead in! They were quite old and tatty, but I hoped that Harriet wouldn't notice.

Mum did! Well, she noticed the jeans.

"You're wearing your new trousers!" she said. "I thought you were keeping those for the party?"

"I'll probably wear a dress for the party," I said. "I might get a bit hot in these."

"You'll get a bit hot in them today! It's going to be well over 20 degrees. If I were you, I'd go and put some shorts on."

110

I couldn't go to tea with Harriet wearing *shorts*. I had this sudden great urge to tell Mum what I was doing, but I knew that I couldn't. Mum is such a worrier! She might even tell me that I wasn't to go. In any case, I had promised Annie not to say anything, and I couldn't break my promise. Not when it was her birthday present to me, and she had worked so hard at it.

"Well, it's up to you," said Mum. "Wear what you like, I don't have time to argue! Now, I'll be picking you up at 6.30 tonight, OK? So you'll be having tea with Annie."

With Harriet, I thought; and I couldn't help a little giggle bursting out of me. Oops! I promptly clapped a hand to my mouth.

"You're in a very odd mood," said Mum. "What's brought all this on?"

"I'll tell you about it later," I said.

"Why can't you tell me now?"

"'Cos I can't! It's a secret."

"I suppose Annie's in on it?"

I said, "Yes, but we're sworn to utter silence."

"Oh! Well... in that case," said Mum.

She didn't try to get it out of me. I am allowed to have secrets! She just told me to eat up my breakfast or I'd make her late for work.

Needless to say I spent the morning jittering, in case for once Rachel didn't go off to gaze at Tyrone and make sure her best friend wasn't pinching him.

"What'd we do? If she doesn't go? How'd we get out?"

"We could always climb through the window," said Annie.

I ran across to look. It's true there is an apple tree outside Annie's window, but I knew I'd never be able to reach it. Heights make me go dizzy. And Annie has *never* been able to get more than a quarter of the way up the ropes when we do gym.

"We'd break our necks," I wailed.

"I wasn't serious," said Annie. "I only said it 'cos of all the dithering you do."

"But Rachel," I moaned.

"You don't have to worry about Rachel. She couldn't stay away from Ty*rone* if you offered her a million dollars. I heard her on the phone last night. She's got it so bad she couldn't even say his name without stuttering... T-T-Ty*rone!*"

"I hope you're right," I said.

"I'm always right," said Annie. "I'm your fairy godmother. When I wave my magic wand—" she snatched up a ruler from her desk and wafted it about "—all your wishes come true!"

She was right about Rachel. She isn't always right; she is sometimes spectacularly *wrong*. But in this case she was right! Rachel came upstairs a bit later, when we were sitting good as gold, quiet as mice, with the CD player turned low as low could be, to tell us that she was going out for a couple of hours.

"You two just behave yourselves—"

"Or else," said Annie.

"Yes! *Or else*. And keep that music down!"

What cheek! We couldn't have turned it any lower if we'd tried.

"Some people are just never satisfied," grumbled Annie.

A few seconds later the front door slammed shut.

"Now we can listen properly," said Annie; and she turned the CD player up to practically full blast. "Let's go and spy on her!"

We raced along the landing, into Annie's mum and dad's bedroom, which is at the front of the house.

"Hide behind the curtain! We don't want her to see us."

Giggling, I wrapped myself up in the curtain and watched as Rachel set off down the road.

"We'll just give her time to get her bus," said Annie. "We don't want to go and bump into her at the bus stop."

Help! I hadn't thought of that! Suppose the bus was cancelled? Suppose we got there and she was still waiting?

"Oh, shut up!" said Annie, when I said this to her. "You're behaving like your mum."

Well! The last thing anyone wants to do is behave like their mum, so I obediently kept quiet and just worried silently inside my head, instead of out loud.

"You're still doing it," said Annie.

"Doing what?" I said.

"*Flapping*. I can tell from just looking at you."

"Well, but you don't think—"

"No, I don't," said Annie, without even waiting to hear what it was that I was going to say. "I've got it all *planned*.

Just leave it to me." She looked at her watch. "Every quarter of an hour. That's when the buses run. We'll go in *quarter of an hour*."

Unlike me, Annie hadn't bothered to get dressed up. She was wearing the same pink joggers she'd been wearing all week, though she had put on a clean top and a big old swanky cap (all pink and puffy) that she's had for ages. But that was all right! It wasn't Annie's birthday treat. She wasn't Harriet's number one fan.

"I'll just do a note for old Bossyboots," she said.

She showed me what she'd written: WE HAVE GONE TO HAVE TEA WITH HARRIET CHANCE. WE WILL BE BACK SOON.

"*Annieeee!*" I stared at her, reproachfully. "I thought we weren't supposed to tell anyone?"

"I've got to leave her a note," said Annie. "We don't want her getting in a panic and phoning the police."

"But you promised!"

Annie stuck out her lower lip. What I call her stubborn look.

"Annie, you *promised*," I said.

"OK! I'll write another one."

WE HAVE GONE TO TEA WITH HARRIET. WE WILL BE BACK SOON.

"How's that? If I just say *Harriet*?"

I told her that that was much better. "It'll keep her from worrying, but she won't actually know where we've gone."

"Right. So now will you please just stop *flapping*?"

I was still a bit scared what we might find when we got to the bus stop. If Rachel was there, we would have to hide in a shop doorway until after she'd gone. Then we'd miss our bus! Harriet would be kept waiting. She would be so cross – it would be so rude! I couldn't bear it!

But then we got there, and I breathed this huge sigh of relief. Rachel was nowhere to be seen!

"Told you so," said Annie. "All that flapping and fussing!"

"I can't help it," I said. "It's my anatomy."

"Your *what*?"

I hesitated. Perhaps I'd got the wrong word. "It's the way I'm made. You can't help the way you're made."

"You don't have to give in to it," said Annie. "When you feel a worry fit coming on, just think, *everything will be all right... Annie says so!*"

I muttered that it hadn't been all right when we'd fallen out of the stationery cupboard, but at that moment our bus came and Annie didn't hear me. Which was probably just as well.

All the way into town my heart was hammering, but now it was with excitement, not worry! I had a tiny touch of anxiety when we reached Market Square, for really no reason at all, but as soon as we were safely on the number six bus, headed for Brafferton Bridge, it disappeared. I suppose I could have started worrying about pile-ups, or being hijacked, but even I am not that sad.

However... when the bus stopped at Brafferton Bridge, and we got out, and there wasn't anyone there to meet us, my heart stopped hammering and went *flomp!* like a dead fish inside my rib cage. I could see that even Annie was a bit concerned.

"Don't worry, don't worry," she said. "She'll be here!"

The bus went on its way, leaving us all by ourselves. Stranded! In the middle of absolutely nowhere.

There aren't any houses at Brafferton Bridge. No one actually lives there. It is just this old ancient bridge over a stream, with fields stretching out on either side as far as the eye can see.

"She'll *be* here," said Annie.

Even as Annie spoke, a red car drew up beside us and a woman got out. It had to be Harriet! She was holding a copy of *Victoria Plum*. A very old, battered copy, like my one of *Candyfloss* before Mum had replaced it. She came over to us, smiling.

"Oh!" she said. "There are two of you! I hadn't realised you were both coming."

I glanced anxiously at Annie. It takes a LOT to make Annie feel uncomfortable, but I could see she was a bit thrown. After all, she was the one who'd set everything up. In any case, I wouldn't have been brave enough to come by myself.

"I th-thought it was w-what we'd arranged," mumbled Annie.

"Of course! That's all right. Two of you is lovely! So which one is the birthday girl?"

Annie beamed and shoved me forward. "Megan! She's your number-one fan."

Harriet held out a hand. "Happy birthday, Megan! Sorry I'm late. I hope you haven't been waiting long?"

I shook my head. I wanted to say, "No, we only just got here," but I couldn't. I was suddenly struck dumb! I could feel my cheeks turning hot tomato. It was Annie who assured her that we had only that minute got off the bus.

"Thank heavens for that! I had visions of you giving up and going back home."

"Wild horses wouldn't get Megan back home," said Annie. "She's been, like, *oh-my-goodness help-help I-can't-believe-it* ever since we set out!"

By now, my cheeks were starting to sizzle. It was just too embarrassing!

"Well, let's get you into the car," said Harriet, "and we'll all go back and have some tea. Who wants to come in front? Megan?"

Annie gave me another shove. "Go on! It's your treat." She then added, beaming, that "Megan always gets sick if she sits in the back."

I don't know why she found it necessary to say that. Getting car sick is such a childish thing to do! But Harriet was really sympathetic. She said, "Oh, join the club! I always had to take pills if I was going a long journey."

"Megs has to stick her head out of the window," said Annie. "Even then it doesn't always stop her throwing up. One time she did it and it all went *splat* down the door. D'you remember?" She leaned forward, chummily, from the back seat. "That time we went to Alton Towers with Mum and Dad?"

I did remember, but I didn't particularly want to be reminded of it. Not in front of Harriet!

"We'd been eating *sardine sandwiches*," said Annie.

"Oh, horrible! Sardine sandwiches aren't at all the right thing to eat if you suffer from car sickness. But don't worry, Megan! There are some peppermints in the glove compartment. They'll help."

"She doesn't usually get sick in front," carolled Annie. "The worst things are those things at fairgrounds that go round and round."

Harriet looked puzzled. "Roundabouts?"

"No, those things where you stick to the side."

"Oh! You mean, like a centrifuge."

"Yes. She gets *really* sick in those!"

"Poor Megan!" Harriet smiled at me as she started the car. "You're obviously like me, you have a delicate stomach."

"You could write a story about someone like that." Annie draped herself, eagerly, over the back of Harriet's seat. "Someone who throws up everywhere she goes... you could call it *Sickly Susan*!"

"Well, it's an idea," said Harriet. "I'll certainly bear it in mind."

She was only being polite; she never used other people's ideas. I knew that, from my reading. She'd said she had "a resistance" to them. I felt like telling Annie to just be quiet. She'd done nothing but burble ever since Harriet had met us! But something had happened to my tongue; it was like a great wodge of foam rubber in my mouth. I couldn't talk! It was really annoying. Although I am not as bubbly and up-front as Annie, I am not usually shy; but when you are in the presence of greatness it is all too easy to just shrivel. Yet I had so many things I wanted to say! So many questions I wanted to ask! Anyone would have thought it was Annie who was the number-one fan rather than me.

"So how long have you been reading my books?" said Harriet.

I whispered, "Since I was about... s-seven."

"She's read them all!" crowed Annie.

"I haven't read them *all*," I said.

"Most of them!"

"Have you read this one?" said Harriet. She pointed at her old battered copy of *Victoria Plum*.

"Yes!" I found it a bit easier, now that we were talking about books. "It's one of my favourites, 'cos Victoria's always having bad hair days. I like the bit where she tries to make it curly and she goes to bed in rollers and says it's like sleeping on a hedgehog!"

"And then she goes to school," – Annie just couldn't resist joining in – "and is forced to play *hockey*, ugh, yuck! And it rains, and all the curls come out!"

"And she says how for a little while she'd looked like a bubble bath but now she's gone back to being a limp dish mop, and she's just so ashamed she runs away and hides in the loo!"

"We used to think that maybe you had hair like a limp dish mop," said Annie. "But you haven't! You've got *nice* hair."

Harriet's hair was beautifully thick and curly – but it was going grey. Harriet was going grey! I felt sad about that, though I knew, of course, she couldn't still look the same as she had fifteen years ago. She was wearing glasses, too. Just for a moment I wished that I could have met her when she was young; but then I thought that that was a very ageist thing to think, and very ungrateful. After all, she was still Harriet. She was still writing wonderful, marvellous books! And she did look warm and friendly; just a bit... mumsy. But that was quite comforting, in a way. If she had been young and glamorous I would probably have been struck dumb for all eternity.

Rather timidly, I said, "How did you manage to know what it's like, having limp hair?"

"Megan's got limp hair," said Annie. "She's always going on about it."

"Like Victoria," I said. "I really love the way you understand how people *feel*. Like having bad hair, or spots, or being plump, or not having any boobs. Like Sugar Mouse. I don't know how you do it!"

"Well... there is such a thing as imagination," said Harriet. "Very important, if you want to be a writer!"

"Megan wants to be a writer," said Annie.

"In that case," said Harriet, "I very much hope that you will be. Do you have a copy of this one, by the way?"

"She's got all of them," said Annie.

"I haven't got *all* of them." Annie did exaggerate so! "You've got a whole shelf full."

"I've got thirty-four," I said.

"Good heavens!" Harriet laughed. "You *are* a fan, aren't you?"

I nodded, bashfully. "*Victoria Plum* was one of the first ones I had."

"And I bet it's in better condition than this! I'm afraid this one's been read to bits."

I have read my copy over and over, but I do try to look after my books and keep them nice. I was only young when I ruined *Candyfloss*. Now that I'm older I wouldn't ever turn down the corners of pages or stand mugs of hot chocolate on them or leave them out in the rain. Poor *Victoria Plum* looked as if all those things had happened to her. I picked her up, and opened her at the title page. Across the top someone had written, "For Jan, with all my love, Mummy". I wondered who Jan was, and why she didn't take better care of her books. Maybe she was Harriet's niece and knew that she could always ask for new ones. It made me feel quite jealous. Imagine having a famous writer as your aunt!

"Hey, look, Megs." Annie lunged forward and poked a finger at me. "Isn't that where we went when we visited your gran?"

Annie had come with me a couple of times, to visit Gran. Mum had thought she would be company for me, but then she had said we couldn't behave ourselves properly, and made too much noise, and upset the old people, so now I had to go on my own.

"Megan's gran is in a home," said Annie. "She has Oldheimer's."

"Alzheimer's," I said.

"Oh, dear! That must be very upsetting," said Harriet.

I said, "Yes, it is, 'cos me and Gran used to be best friends. Now she doesn't even know me... like Clover's gran, in *Daisy & Clover*. I cried when I read the bit where Clover wants to burst into tears. That's just how I feel, when I see Gran... you always seem to be writing about how I feel! Like when Clover says about remembering all the things that she and her gran used to do together—"

"That was me," said Harriet, "remembering *my* gran! She had Alzheimer's, too. That's what made me want to write about it."

"Except that... Clover's gran doesn't actually have *Alzheimer's*," I said.

"She has a stroke," said Annie.

"Oh! Well, yes. I changed it to a stroke for the purposes of the book. It would have been too painful," said Harriet, "actually writing about Alzheimer's. It would have brought back too many memories. So you know this area quite well, do you, Megan?"

"Only from coming to see Gran," I said. "Over there's where we get off the bus."

"Darnley Manor. A very pleasant spot! We're just a few miles further on. Are you feeling all right? Not getting sick?"

"She doesn't give you any warning," said Annie. "She just opens her mouth and does it... *blurgh*! All over the door."

Annie doesn't say these things on purpose to embarrass me. She just opens *her* mouth and words come tumbling out. Mostly I try not to mind.

"Well, just yell," said Harriet, "if you want to stop. We've got a few twisty turny bits coming up. They're always the worst, if you have a funny tum."

I thought that Harriet was so nice! Every bit as understanding as she seemed from her books. A girl at school had once met this other author she was keen on and said she had turned out to be really cold and snooty. A huge disappointment! Harriet wasn't in the least bit snooty. Or cold. She was just like one of us.

"I'll tell you what," she said, "I must just quickly ring home and… bother!" She was rummaging with one hand in her bag. "Would you believe it, I've gone and forgotten my mobile! Honestly, I'd leave my head behind if it weren't attached to my shoulders! I don't suppose either of you has one I could borrow?"

I said, "I do!" I felt quite honoured, offering my phone to Harriet! "You can use mine."

128

"Bless you!" Harriet slammed the glove compartment shut and blew me a kiss. "You've saved my bacon. I should have rung half an hour ago! I'll just pull up in this lay-by... mustn't use a mobile while you're driving. Very dangerous!"

I thought that Mum would approve of that. When we had gone to Alton Towers – the time I got sick and it sprayed over the door. On the *outside*, I should add – Annie's dad had done lots of talking on his mobile. Mum had said afterwards that she hadn't liked to say anything, as it wasn't her car, but she had been on tenterhooks the whole time. So that was ten out of ten for Harriet. Hooray!

I felt very privileged and important, sitting next to a famous author as she rang home. I wondered who she was going to talk to. Could it be Lori? I knew it wouldn't be her husband 'cos I'd read somewhere that she was divorced.

Harriet pulled a face. "Answerphone... I hate when it's the answerphone!"

Me, too. I knew how she felt. Sometimes if I get an answerphone I just hang up, though I know it's a bit rude and you ought really to say who you are and leave a message, which was what Harriet was doing.

"Darling, where are you? This is Mummy here! Where have you gone?" She sounded a bit upset. I guessed that Lori had gone off without telling her. "Can you hear me? Are you listening? Please speak to me! If you're there… please! Pick up!"

Just for a moment it was like really tense. Even Annie must have felt it. She leaned forward intently across the back of the seat as we waited for Lori to pick up the phone. But she didn't.

"Call me," whispered Harriet. "Please, darling, call me!"

After that there was this long silence, and then she gave a little laugh, sort of half ashamed, like pulling herself together, and said, "Oh, dear! Mothers do worry so. Does your mother worry, Megan?"

I said that she did.

"Megan's mum gets into total flaps," said Annie.

"I'm afraid I do, too. You just never know… what might have happened… " Harriet's voice faded out.

Trying to be helpful, I said, "Couldn't you try her mobile?"

"Her mobile? No, she doesn't have a mobile. If only she had had a mobile. She's not answering… she doesn't answer… I hope you have your mobile with you, Annie?"

Annie confessed that she hadn't. "We came out in such a rush. I think it's on the kitchen table."

"That's naughty! What would you do if Megan's ran out?"

"Find a call box," said Annie.

"Not good enough! You should always take your phone with you. If only—" Harriet stopped. "Well, anyway!" she said. "Let's get on. I'm so sorry if I'm sounding a bit vague, but I'm in the middle of writing a new book and it's going round and round in my head."

"What's it called?" said Annie. "Has it got a title?"
"Um... yes. How about... *Jampot Jane*?"

I giggled. Annie, in her bold way, said, "That's a funny title! What's it about?"

"I'm afraid I can't tell you that," said Harriet. "I never discuss my books before they're published!"

I hoped that Annie felt properly put in her place. Such nosiness! It was one thing to be a fan, and to show interest; but to poke and pry was just bad manners.

"I'll keep the phone by me, Megan, if I may," said Harriet, "just in case. And I'll try to stop thinking about work and concentrate on you, instead. This is your birthday treat, and I want you to enjoy it."

RACHEL'S DIARY (THURSDAY)

I am just so absolutely ANNOYED. That little fat freak and her skinny little friend have gone and done a runner. They have had the NERVE to leave me a note. Gone to tea with Harriet, whoever Harriet is. How dare they??? They know perfectly well they're not supposed to go off without telling me. They'd better just get back before Mum comes home or we shall all be in trouble. AND it hasn't taken its phone with it. What's the point of having a mobile if it's just going to leave it lying around on the kitchen table when it goes out? It shouldn't be out! It's just taking a mean advantage. It thinks it can get away with it because I daren't tell Mum. It's a rotten thing to do! It knows how I feel about Ty.

Oh, and I was so happy! It's Jem's day off so me and Ty had lunch together, all by ourselves. He's going to call round at seven on Saturday, to take me to the party. Jem is going as well, with Kieron, so it should be lots of fun. I wasn't a bit tongue-tied today, on my own with Ty. We just have so many things in  common. So many things to talk about! We are both into sport in a big way, are both huge fans of Man U, and our ace fave band is Hot Brits. So no embarrassing pauses while I rack my brain trying to think what to say! We could just go on for ever. I think it's truly important that when you are attracted to someone it should be more than merely physical. Ty is gorgeous — but we can TALK. For instance we had this really in-depth discussion about our aims and ambitions. Not just to stack shelves from now till the end of time! Ty is thinking of going into the army, but I am trying to persuade him to join the police. He is definitely interested!

In the meantime, I WAS going to go and try things on ready for Saturday. I have to look my best!!! But now I'm too cross and angry, because of the

Scumbag taking advantage. She might at least have given me a telephone number. I bet she didn't on purpose. I bet that's why she left her phone, as well, so I couldn't get hold of her. Then she'll pretend she just forgot. It's such a scummy thing to do! I'm surprised at the Stick Insect; I should have thought she'd know better. She always comes across like butter wouldn't melt in her mouth, and for an eleven-year-old she is quite sensible, on the whole. Unlike my dear little sister, who is just one great big PAIN.

To think that out of the goodness of my heart, because I was feeling so happy, I actually brought back some cakes for tea! Squidgy ones full of cream, as a special treat, to make up for yelling at her about the music. I think I'll try ringing Jem and see if she feels like coming over and helping me eat them. Then we can go through my wardrobe together and decide what I'm going to wear. I am NOT going to worry myself about little Tubby Scumbag. She is old enough to know better, and I don't see why I should.

Six

WE DROVE ON through the countryside, down lots of twisty turny lanes, just like Harriet had said. I opened the window and ate peppermints and didn't get sick, but it did seem a long way to drive. Well, to me it did. I thought probably it was because I wasn't used to car journeys. Mum can't afford a car, so we don't really travel very much. It obviously didn't bother Annie. She was bouncing all over the place like a rubber ball. She kept suddenly appearing over the back of my seat and poking at me.

"Hey, look! There's a rabbit!" "Oh, look! Donkeys!" "Look, look! Lambs!"

"Yes, we're way out in the country now," said Harriet.

Rather shyly, not wanting it to seem like I was prying, I said, "I thought you lived in London?"

"Oh! Yes. London's where I *live*. But in the country is where I write my books. Not many people know where I do my writing! I like to keep it a secret."

She explained how nothing was worse, when you were concentrating really hard, and trying to think what to write next, than to have people come knocking at the door expecting to be invited in for a cup of tea, or ringing you up "just for a chat".

I knew how she felt. It was what I sometimes feel when I'm writing an essay for school and Mum says, "Megan, put that away now, it's time for tea." I always wail, "Mum, I can't stop in the middle of something!" But Mum never understands, because Mum isn't a writer. By the time I've had tea and gone back to my essay, I have totally forgotten what I was going to write. I said this to Harriet, and she said, "Oh, you understand! We are obviously on the same wavelength."

I just, like, *glowed*. I felt so proud at being taken into Harriet's confidence! If I hadn't been in the car I would

 have written things down in my reporter's book that I had brought with me; but I can't write – or read – in cars, because of car sickness. However, I knew that I wouldn't forget it. It was something that Harriet and I had in common. We were both writers! And we didn't like to be disturbed.

"This was another reason," said Harriet, "why I didn't want you telling anyone about our secret meeting... if readers discovered my hideaway, it would be the end! I'd never have a moment's peace. I would have to move."

Earnestly, I assured her that we hadn't told a soul. "And we won't. I promise!" I then turned round and pulled a face at Annie, 'cos Annie very nearly *had* told.

"Wouldn't have made any difference," said Annie.

"What's that?" said Harriet. "What wouldn't have made any difference?"

"If I'd told my sister we were coming to meet you."

"But she didn't!" I said, quickly. "I stopped her."

"Good girl," said Harriet.

"She still wouldn't have known where you lived," said Annie.

"She might have found out," I said.

"Well, she probably wouldn't have been able to," said Harriet, "because not even my publishers have my country address. I don't give my country address to anyone! It's my very secret hideaway where I can be private."

"Even from Lori?" I said.

"Lori? Oh, no not from Lori. of course not. But from the rest of the world… You have no idea what it's like to be constantly bombarded by total strangers turning up on the doorstep wanting autographs, or wanting books signed, or just to come in for a chat."

"It must be horrible!" I said. I really meant it. I wouldn't want to be a celeb! Annie, however, said she thought it would be quite fun.

"It might seem so, just at first," said Harriet, "but in the end it wears you down."

"That's right," I said. "You want to write books, not keep on being bothered all the time."

"Oh, Megan! You and I are kindred spirits," said Harriet. Which made me glow all over again!

We finally reached what Harriet called her secret hideaway.

"Wasn't there some writer," she said, "who had a shed in the garden?"

"Roald Dahl," I said.

"Roald Dahl! I knew it was someone famous. He had his shed, I have my cottage."

The cottage was at the bottom of a narrow lane. The lane ended up in a woody area, with a field on one side. It was rutted and bumpy, and hardly wide enough for a car.

"Sorry for the rough ride," said Harriet, as we jolted and bounced. "Not many people come down here – which is why I love it so! Complete peace and quiet."

"Don't you get lonely?" said Annie.

"Lonely? Not at all! How could I get lonely when I have all my characters for company?"

"I would," said Annie.

"You're not a writer," I said.

Harriet's hideaway was like a little dolls' house. Really cute! Harriet apologised for the fact that it was a bit tumbledown. She said, "It needs a lot of work done on it, but it's such an upheaval!"

"It's like the one in Hansel and Gretel," said Annie.

"The witch's cottage? Was that tumbledown?"

"No, but it was kind of... spooky."

"Annieee!" I was horrified. How could she be so rude? "It's not spooky, it's lovely!"

I thought that if I were writing a description of it for English, I would say that it was *picturesque*. Just right for an author!

"I always have to watch my head," said Harriet, ducking as she opened the door.

The door gave straight on to the sitting room, which was quite bare. Just a chair and table, and an old saggy sofa. No books! That surprised me, but Harriet explained that if she had books there she would keep breaking off to read them.

"I am so easily distracted! I have a mind like a flea."

140

I was a bit puzzled by this as I had once read how Harriet Chance liked to sit at her kitchen table and write her first draft by hand, surrounded by her four cats. Surely cats would distract her? The lady who lives downstairs from us has a cat called Biddy, and when she comes to visit us, Biddy I mean, she always spreads herself out across my homework, if I'm doing homework, and starts grooming herself or purring. I find that very distracting!

I told this to Harriet. "Sometimes," I said, "she even tries to chew the paper!"

"Oh, I couldn't be doing with that," said Harriet. "I couldn't write with cats around! And I couldn't write on paper... far too slow!"

Falteringly, I said, "I read this interview where you said how you always did your first draft by hand... you said you couldn't write straight on to a computer."

"Did I?" She laughed. "Well, I've been dragged kicking and screaming into the twenty-first century! One has to move with the times."

"I still write by hand," I said.

"That's only 'cos you don't have a computer," said Annie.

"They are one of the blessings of modern technology," said Harriet. "Imagine! If I didn't have a computer, we would never have met. Now, then! How about some tea? Annie, clear a space on the table while I go and get it."

I needed to go to the loo – I always do after a car journey. Harriet told me the bathroom was "directly ahead, up the stairs... but be warned, it's a bit primitive!"

It was such a funny little place, the bathroom. Like a little cell. All it had was a washbasin and a toilet, with a cracked bit of mirror on the wall. Both the washbasin and the toilet were very old-fashioned. The washbasin was propped up on a sort of iron stand, and the toilet had a long chain with a handle that you had to pull when you'd finished. The toilet had a broken seat, and a long chain with a handle that you had to pull when you'd finished, except that it didn't seem to work, which was rather embarrassing. Red-faced, I told Harriet about it, and she said, "Oh, dear! Never mind. At least it's better than having to go outside... imagine that on a dark night!"

"You could write a book about someone living in a place like this," said Annie. "You could call it *Spooky Cottage*."

I cringed, but Harriet said, "Do you know, that's a really good idea? I might well do that! And then I could dedicate it to you both. *To Annie and Megan, who came to tea.* Speaking of which—" she whisked away a cloth which was covering the table. "How about that?"

I gasped. I couldn't believe it! It was like a fairy tale... all my favourite food was there! A bowl full of tiny weeny Easter eggs – another bowl full of Cadbury's Creme ones – a *big* bowl of crisps – a plate of ham sandwiches and a baby birthday cake, with twelve candles crowded on the top.

"This was *our* secret," gloated Annie. "I told Harriet all the stuff you loved to eat!"

"I hope we got it right," said Harriet.

"We did!" said Annie. "She adores all this stuff!"

I'm afraid it is true. It is exactly the sort of food that I would like to have on a desert island. The sort of food that Mum only lets me eat in what Gran would have called "dribs and drabs". Certainly not all in one go!

"Fortunately," said Harriet, "I bought enough to feed an army, so get stuck in, the pair of you."

Annie and I sat munching side by side on the saggy sofa. Harriet sat at the table. I was quite surprised to see that she was eating ham sandwiches as I had once read that she was a vegetarian; but I thought perhaps she was only doing it to be polite, what with me being a guest, and so I didn't say anything. It would have seemed ungracious.

After we'd eaten as much as we could, and I'd blown out the candles on the cake and made a birthday wish – even though it wasn't yet properly my birthday – I settled down with my reporter's notebook to interview Harriet. Annie kept nagging to know what I'd wished for, but Harriet told her that birthday wishes had to be secret, "Otherwise they won't come true."

Annie said, "Will you tell me if it *does* come true?"

I said, "Yes, but it won't be for ages yet!" Not unless you could have books published and get famous while you were still at school... Was that possible? I opened my notepad and wrote it down, as a question to ask Harriet. I had a long list of questions! I had carefully worked them all out in advance. I had decided there wasn't any point asking her things I already had the answers to, so I'd tried to think of questions she maybe hadn't been asked before. This was my list:

Questions for Harriet Chance

What was Paper Dolls about?

What was your grown-up book about and what was it called?

In Scarlet Feather, does Scarlet choose to go with her mum or her dad?

Were you ever like any of your characters when you were young? If so, which ones?

Have you ever written a book using an idea that was given to you by someone else?

What made you decide to become a vegetarian?

Do you think a person could have a book published while they were still at school?

"Right! You come and sit at the table," said Harriet, "I'll sit on the sofa with Annie. Now! Fire away."

I cleared my throat. "Can you tell me what your book *Paper Dolls* was about?"

"*Paper Dolls?* Oh! Well... it was about paper dolls. Is that one you haven't read?"

"It was the one you wrote when you were at s-school," I said. "It... it wasn't ever published."

"Oh, good heavens, you're right!" Harriet banged a clenched fist to her forehead. "Silly of me! Memory like a sieve. But it was definitely about paper dolls. I used to play with them, when I was a child."

Dutifully, I wrote it down. I wasn't quite sure what a paper doll was, but I didn't want to bore Harriet by asking too many questions, especially silly ones.

"Sorry about that," said Harriet. "But I was at school a very long time ago!"

"That's all right," I said. "What about your grown-up book that you wrote?"

"Ah, yes," said Harriet. "My grown-up book."

"What was that about?"

"Um... well! It was... you know!" She waved a hand. "Best not talked about."

I thought perhaps she meant that it was rude.

All about sex, or maybe drugs.

"Not the sort of thing you'd want to read," she said. "Next question!"

"In *Scarlet Feather*, when Scarlet's mum and dad split up, which of them does Scarlet choose to go and live with?"

Harriet hesitated. "That's not fair!" shrilled Annie. "You shouldn't ask the ending of a book before you've read it!"

"No, you certainly should not," said Harriet.

"It's cheating! Don't tell her!"

"I don't intend to," said Harriet. "But it was a good try!"

"I just wanted to get a scoop," I said. "Like in the newspapers."

"But if you give all my plots away, no one will bother to buy the books!"

I hadn't thought of that.

"Next question!"

I consulted my list. "Were you ever like any of your characters when you were young, and if so, which ones?"

"Oh, dear! That's asking."

"You don't have to tell me if you don't want," I said. "It's just that you always seem to know how people feel. Like Victoria Plum and her hair. And Sugar Mouse and—"

"Sugar Mouse! That was me. That was my nickname, when I was at school... Mouse. Because I was so mouse-like! Wouldn't say boo to a goose. You probably wouldn't think it now," said Harriet, "but I was just so shy! Always scuttling off into the corner." She made little scuttling motions with her hands. "So, yes, you're right! I know all about being mouse-like."

There was a bit of a silence.

"Well, aren't you going to write it down?" said Annie.

I swallowed, and started writing. Perhaps *Sugar Mouse* was one that Annie hadn't read. Or perhaps she'd forgotten it. It seemed like Harriet had forgotten it, too. Sugar Mouse doesn't get her nickname because she's mouse-like, she gets it because she dances the *part* of a sugar mouse in the end-of-term show at her ballet school. She's chosen because she's very tiny and dainty. But she's also very perky and up-front! She has people in stitches doing really wicked imitations of her ballet teacher. She's not mouse-like at all.

It was worrying how Harriet didn't seem able to remember things. It reminded me of Gran, and her Alzheimer's. But Harriet was too young to have Alzheimer's! And she didn't behave like Gran used to behave. She didn't suddenly stop speaking, and look lost, or go out of the room to fetch one thing and come back with another. She seemed absolutely totally normal, except for not being able to remember the characters in her own books.

Maybe that was what happened when you wrote a lot of books? Maybe you forgot what you'd written in them? It was a bit disappointing, as I'd been looking forward to asking lots of questions about my favourite characters; but I reminded myself that I was really lucky to be here at all.

"So how are we doing?" said Harriet. "Got any more?"

"J-just t-two," I said. I decided I wouldn't bother asking her the one I'd added, about getting books published while you were at school. I didn't want to wear her out.

"Right, then! Let's be having them."

I seemed to have a ping-pong ball in my throat. I swallowed, and forced it back down.

"Have you ever written a book using an idea that's been given to you by someone else?"

I expected her to say a very firm no, because of what I'd read. If she'd have said no, I was going to ask her *why* she had resistance. But she didn't say no. She said yes! She said, "Yes, yes, absolutely! People are always giving me ideas. It's very important to listen when people tell you things. They have such extraordinary stories! Things you couldn't possibly make up. They give you all sorts of wonderful ideas!"

"Like *Spooky Cottage*," said Annie.

"Exactly! Yes!"

Maybe, I thought, the person who had interviewed her before had got it wrong. It was the only explanation.

"So which books," I said, "have come from ideas that other people have given you?"

"Oh... loads of them! That one." She pointed at the battered copy of *Victoria Plum*. "I had a friend with limp hair. She was always having bad hair days. So I put her in a book!"

I was sure I'd read that it was Harriet herself who had bad hair days and limp hair, and *that* was why she wrote the book. But she didn't have limp hair, she had lovely thick curly hair, even though it was going grey. It was really difficult, knowing what to think. Maybe she had just pretended it was based on herself. Authors probably did that sort of thing.

Now I had only one question left.

"What made you decide to become a vegetarian?"

I had blurted it out before I could stop myself. I went red as soon as I'd said it. Harriet went a bit red, too.

"Oh, dear!" she said. "You've properly caught me out, haven't you?"

151

I hadn't meant to. I didn't want to embarrass her! "It's just that I r-read somewhere that you were a v-vegetarian—"

"And now I've been caught red-handed, eating ham sandwiches! Well, that's my credibility gone. You'll never trust me again, will you?"

"Sometimes people who are vegetarians eat meat," said Annie.

"Only if they give way to a moment of weakness," said Harriet. "I'm sorry, Megan! Ham sandwiches are my weakness."

I didn't point out that she had said in the interview it was something she felt quite passionately about. It seemed that you couldn't rely on interviews. Either the people that did the interviewing made things up, or... or the people that were being interviewed didn't always tell the truth. I just didn't know what to believe!

"Is that the lot?" said Harriet. "Have you finished grilling me? Good! In that case—" she reached out for her bag, which was on the floor beside her. "I have a birthday present for you. Here!"

She handed me a book-shaped package. Just for a moment my heart leapt, as I thought perhaps it might be a copy of *Scarlet Feather*; but I knew at once it wasn't heavy enough for a hardback. I tore off the wrapping, and there inside was an old dog-eared copy of... *Patsy Puffball*! Harriet Chance's very first book. The one she was ashamed of, and would like all copies of it destroyed. In 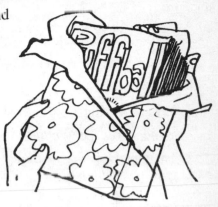 spite of that, I was quite pleased to have it, because it was one I'd never been able to find.

"I'm afraid it's only second-hand," said Harriet. "I wish I could have found a good copy for you, but after all this time I don't have any left. If you look at the publication date, you'll see that it's very old."

Obediently, I looked. Inside were the words, "For Jan on her birthday, with love from Mummy xxx." And then, inside the front cover: "Janis Patmore: her book."

"You don't already have it, do you?"

"N-no." I shook my head "No, I don't. Thank you very much!"

"You're welcome. It may be an early work," said Harriet, "but it's one I'm still proud of! That's why I just couldn't resist, when I saw it going second-hand. I had to rescue it!"

"So you – you wouldn't want it to be destroyed?" I said.

"Destroyed? Good heavens, no! Why should I want it to be destroyed?"

"Like if, perhaps, you thought it wasn't very good?"

Annie said, "Meg*annnnn*!"

"Like maybe if you thought your later books were better?"

"Well, I'm sure they are," said Harriet. "In fact, I should hope they are! This must be one of the very first books I ever wrote."

"It was," I said; and I could hear my voice, all small and tight. "It was the *very* first."

There was a pause.

"The first to be published," I said.

"Oh, goodness! Was it really?" said Harriet. "My memory!" She banged her fist against her forehead. "It's getting to be like a leaking bucket! What must you think of me?"

Gravely I said, "That's all right."

"It's not all right! You know more about me than I do!"

Harriet laughed, and so did Annie, but I felt this strange little shiver go prickling down my spine.

"I'll read the book," said Annie, snatching it from me, "if she thinks it's beneath her."

"I didn't *say* that," I said. "I just... I thought... it was a book you didn't like any more!"

"Whatever gave you that idea?" wondered Harriet.

"It was... s-something I read."

"Oh! You don't want to take any notice of things you read. You've probably read all sorts of things. Haven't you?"

"Y-yes." I swallowed, rather desperately. "Actually," I said, "thank you very much for the tea but I think perhaps we ought to go now."

"Go?" Annie glared at me. "What for? We're not in a rush!"

"No, and surely you'd like your photos taken?" said Harriet. "For your project?"

"Yessss!" Annie punched the air, exultantly. She just loves having her photo taken.

"Let me have your address," said Harriet, "and I'll send them on to you."

Annie opened her mouth to blurt out where she lived.
I got in, just in time.

"Really," I said, "it doesn't matter." I knew enough to
know that you never give your address to strangers. And
Harriet *was* a stranger, even if I did love her books.

If they were her books. I was beginning to have the
most horrible doubts.

"We do honestly have to go," I said.

"No, we don't!" said Annie. "We can stay till—" she
looked at her watch – "at least five o'clock."

"Oh, that will give us plenty of time for photographs!
You must have your photographs. After all, it's probably
the only opportunity you'll ever get."

By now I was in a bit of a panic. I just knew that
something wasn't right.

"Please could I ring my mum?" I said.

"Of course you can ring your mum!" said Harriet.
"Where's your phone? Did I leave it in the car? I must
have left it in the car!"

"I'll go and get it," I said.

I made a run for the door, but Harriet got there first.

"No, no! You wait here." She smiled. "I'll go!"

There wasn't anything I could do.

RACHEL'S DIARY (THURSDAY)

I am getting worried. I don't know what to do! I think I'm going to have to ring Mum.

It's just gone four o'clock and Jem has left. There isn't any sign of Annie or Megan. While Jem was here I looked on the computer and found the email addresses of people that I think are in their class at school. People I've heard them talk about. I was hoping there'd be someone called Harriet, but there wasn't. Jem said, "Well, she must be a friend or they wouldn't have gone to tea with her. Haven't they ever mentioned anyone called Harriet?"

I thought about it, and I said maybe they had. It did sound sort of familiar.

"In that case, it's obviously a friend that doesn't have email," said Jem. She suggested I try ringing up some of the other people and seeing if they knew who she was, which I thought was a good idea. I took a couple of people off the computer, ones with unusual surnames, Ravjani and Caldecott, that I thought there couldn't be too many of, and looked them up in the local directory. I got through to both of them. They were both in Annie's class but they said they didn't know anyone called Harriet. There wasn't any Harriet in Year Seven.

There aren't any in our year, either. There aren't any in the netball teams, or the hockey teams, or the gym squad. There aren't any prefects called Harriet. There isn't ANYONE called Harriet, that I can think of.

Jem could see that I was starting to grow a bit agitated. She knows I'll be in trouble if Mum finds out about me going off and leaving them every day.

"Clues," said Jem. "She might have had a letter, or something."

"She doesn't get letters," I said.

Jem said well, it wouldn't hurt to look, so between us we ransacked Annie's bedroom. I know bedrooms are private, but it's her own stupid fault! It was Jem who went through the waste paper basket and found the note: HAVE GONE TO HAVE TEA WITH HARRIET CHANCE. Exactly the same as the one she left for me to read, except that my one just says "Harriet". I immediately rushed back downstairs to look up Harriet Chance in the directory. She wasn't there!

"She must be local," I wailed, "if they've gone to have tea with her!"

I'm the one who wants to go into the CID, but it was Jem — AGAIN — who came up with a clue. Well, it seemed like a clue. She suddenly remembered who Harriet Chance was.

"She's a writer!"

Of course, as soon as she said it I realised why the name sounded familiar. I think I read one of her books once. And Megan is like, this really big bookworm. It was all starting to come together! They'd gone to have tea with one of their favourite writers. Now all we had to do was find out where.

"Ring the publisher," said Jem. "Ask where she lives!"

I'd have thought of it myself if I hadn't been in such a frazzle. If I was in the CID they wouldn't let me work on a case that I was personally involved in.

We raced back upstairs and into Annie's bedroom. Please, PLEASE, I was thinking, let her have one of the woman's books! She's got this one called Candytuft — Candyfloss. Something like that. Inside it says the name of the publisher, so I at once got the number from Directory Enquiries and rang and asked to speak to "someone who knows about Harriet Chance". I was actually, almost, beginning to feel a bit pleased with myself. I mean I was being really efficient. Really probing. CID, here I come!

All I wanted was an address and telephone number, but they wouldn't give them to me. Not even when I told them how my little sister had gone off to have tea.

"I need to talk to her! It's urgent!"

In the end they put me through to this person called Caroline Something who said she was Harriet Chance's editor. She said she was very sorry, but they didn't give out the addresses of their authors. Or their telephone numbers. Or their email addresses. But I think I rattled her a bit, because after I'd told the story all over again, about Annie going off to have tea, she said that she would get in touch with Harriet Chance herself and ring me back.

I'm still waiting! It's been nearly half an hour. Jem has had to go, and I'm all by myself. I don't know what to do! I ought to ring Mum, but I really don't want to. It's still only four o'clock. They could come back any minute. And when they do, I won't half give them what for! Going off like that, w—

I stopped there, because the telephone rang. I grabbed at it, hoping it would be Annie, but it wasn't. It was the Caroline person. She says she's spoken to Harriet Chance, and Harriet Chance is at home in London doing her writing and doesn't know anything about having tea with my sister. She made me go right through the story for the third time. She kept asking me these questions, like was I sure it was THE Harriet Chance, and had Annie ever had a letter from Harriet Chance, and did she read Harriet Chance's books, and did she ever go into chatrooms. It was only when I said yes about the chatrooms that she kind of went into overdrive and said she thought she'd better get in touch with the police.

Now I wish I'd never rung her! Dad will have a fit if the police suddenly turn up. And anyway, what's the point? They're not MISSING. The little tubby beast has just gone off somewhere on purpose to annoy me and get me into trouble and pay me back for telling her to turn her music down. I know her!

I bet she's gone up to London. I bet she was going to go and have tea with Harriet Chance, and then at the last minute changed her mind. I bet that's what happened.

But why would Harriet Chance say she didn't know anything about it?

Because maybe she didn't know anything about it! Maybe somehow Annie got hold of her address and talked Megan into going with her, and it was going to be a surprise visit. Turn up on the doorstep and get themselves invited in for tea. That would be JUST like Annie. Just the stupid, thoughtless, inconsiderate sort of thing she'd do. And then she'd suddenly have got cold feet, or most likely Megan would. She's more timid than Annie, and she's got a bit more sense. They're probably on their way back right now.

I just hope they turn up before Mum comes home!

seven

THE MINUTE THE door closed, Annie turned on me.

"What's the matter with you? This is meant to be a birthday treat, and you're going and ruining it! Why are you being so horrid, when Harriet's being so nice?"

I said, "Because—"

"Because *what*?"

"Because I don't think it *is* Harriet!"

Annie stared at me like I'd suddenly gone mad. "What d'you mean? Of course it's Harriet! Who else would it be?"

I said, "I d-don't know, but—"

Annie put her hands on her hips and stood there, waiting. "*But?*"

"Something's not right!"

"Like what?"

"Like – she doesn't know things! Things she ought to know. Things she's said—"

"She's just forgotten!"

"She can't have forgotten *everything*. She can't have forgotten her own books!"

Annie frowned.

"She didn't even know that Clover's gran had a stroke," I said. "She thought it was Alzheimer's. And *Sugar Mouse*, she thought she was called that because she was mouse-like! And how could she have forgotten that *Patsy Puffball* was her very first book?"

"Well, I – I don't know! I—"

"She couldn't!" I said. "Nobody could forget their very first book! And that copy of *Victoria Plum* that she bought? She got it second-hand. It's got the same name in it that's in *Patsy Puffball*."

"I don't see that's anything to go by," muttered Annie; but I could see that she was beginning to have doubts by the way her mouth was puckering.

"There's another thing," I said. "Why did she keep my mobile? And why wouldn't she let me go and get it?"

"She didn't actually *stop* you going and getting it. And she did ring Lori!"

"If it really was Lori."

"Well, who else could it have been?"

"Anyone! *No* one. She said it was an answerphone."

"But she left a message! She said, 'This is Mummy'."

"She could just have been pretending."

Annie's voice quivered. "W-what would she do that for?"

"To make us believe that she was Harriet! Don't you see?"

Annie gazed at me, doubtfully.

"She wanted to get hold of my phone." I was remembering how just afterwards she'd ask Annie whether she had her mobile with her and Annie had said no. What would have happened if Annie had said yes? Would she have found some way of getting it off her? Like saying she had to make another call and mine had run out of money, or—

"Megan!" Annie was tugging urgently at my sleeve. "Stop it!"

"I don't think we ought to be here," I said. "I don't think we ought to have come!"

"But... *I* talked to Lori. We had this long conversation! In the bookroom!"

166

"How do you know that it was really her?"

"Well... b-because— " Annie faltered, and came to a stop.

"You don't!" I said. Anyone could pretend to be anyone, in a chatroom.

And anyone could look up Harriet Chance and see what had been written about her, like I had. Except that I had remembered it all; this woman hadn't.

We heard the sound of a key turning in the lock. She was coming back.

"Ask her when Lori's birthday is," I hissed.

"W-why? When is it?"

"New Year's Day. See if she knows."

I knew, because there wasn't anything that had been published about Harriet Chance that I didn't know.

The door creaked open, and Harriet – if it was Harriet – ducked her head and came in. Annie mouthed at me: "Ring your mum!"

"Megan, I'm so sorry," said the woman. She wasn't Harriet! I knew she wasn't. How could I ever have thought she was?

She didn't have Harriet's hair. She didn't know the characters in her own books. She didn't know that she never used other people's ideas. This person wasn't Harriet Chance!

"I'm really sorry," she said. "But your phone has gone dead. You must have forgotten to recharge the battery. You are a naughty girl!"

I felt my cheeks turn crimson. I was sure I hadn't forgotten; Mum was always reminding me.

"C-could I have a look at it?" I said.

"Well, I've left it in the car. It isn't any use, it's completely dead."

"But I need to ring my mum!" I said.

"Oh, dear! What shall we do? Your phone's dead, and Annie and I have left ours behind. How stupid of us. Now your Mum will never know where you are."

That was the moment when I knew for certain sure. Annie and I had made a terrible mistake. I didn't need Annie to suddenly blurt out, "When is your daughter's birthday?" Even if the woman had said "New Year's Day" I still wouldn't have believed she was the real Harriet. But she didn't.

She stared at Annie with these strange glassy eyes and said, "My daughter's birthday? I don't have a daughter…

my daughter is dead. My little girl is dead! That's why she doesn't answer when I ring her… she's not here any more! She's left me!"

Cold, wet
goose feet went
plapping down my
spine. I could feel Annie
trembling beside me and I knew that she was just as terrified as I was.

"You're not my little girl, are you?" The woman turned, slowly, to look at me. "You're just pretending to be her."

"No!" My voice came out in a horrified squawk. "I'm n-not! I'm not pretending!"

"You are. You're trying to make me believe that she's come back to me!"

I tried to swallow, but I couldn't, my throat had gone dry. Next to me, Annie was trembling like a leaf. I knew that we were in the most horrible situation, but I couldn't think how to get out of it. If we ran for the door, the woman would get there before us, and also it might make her angry.

The one thing I knew I mustn't do was panic. I looked at my watch and in this very calm, controlled voice I said, "I really do think we ought to be going now, if you don't mind."

"Going?" said the woman. "Going where?"

"G-going h-home," I said; and I edged desperately towards the door, tugging Annie with me. The woman at once moved across, to block our path.

"What do you mean, you're going home? This is your home!"

"No," I shouted, "it's not! It's not our home, and we don't belong here! We're nothing to do with you?"

"What?" The woman stopped, like someone had plunged a knife into her. She looked totally bewildered then suddenly wrenched open the door and cried, "Go! The pair of you! Go, now! Quickly!"

I didn't wait. I grabbed Annie by the arm and dragged her out of the cottage. I didn't dare use the road, she might follow in the car, so I dragged Annie into the surrounding woods, and together we ran. We ran and we ran, tripping over roots, falling into brambles.

Horrid scratchy things tore at us, overhanging branches nearly poked our eyes out, and still we went on running. I wouldn't let Annie stop. She was sobbing and gasping, with tears rolling down her cheeks and blood streaking her forehead, but I forced her to go on.

It is usually Annie who takes the lead; she is the one who makes the decisions and says what we're going to do. That day, it was me. I ran like I have never run before, with Annie stumbling after me.

I just knew that we had to get as far away from that cottage as we possibly could.

RACHEL'S DIARY (THURSDAY)

Jem has just rung to ask if they are back yet. When I said no, she said why didn't I see if I could find the number for Megan's mobile and try ringing her at it.

I felt so ashamed, because why didn't I think of that? Not that it has done any good. If anything, it has just made matters worse, because I am more worried now than I was before.

I found the number on Mum's telephone pad, but when I rang it there was no reply. It just rang and rang until a recorded voice came on saying that the person I'd called was not available.

I don't know whether this means that Megan has also gone off without her phone, or whether it means she's just not answering. But Megan wouldn't go off without her phone!

And she wouldn't not answer. Not if she heard it ringing. She is such an ORDERED little thing.

This is like a nightmare. The Caroline person rang to say that the police were on their way, so now I'm going to have to ring Mum. I don't care any more if she gets mad at me. I just want them to come back safe!

eight

WELL! SO THAT was my birthday treat. Some treat! Not
that I am blaming Annie, it was every bit as much my
fault as hers. We should both of us have known better. As
Mum says, "You'd been told often enough!" I still don't
know how we could have been so stupid. Stupid, stupid,
STUPID. Even now, after all these months, I really don't
like to think about it. It was just so so frightening. So
really scary. The most scary thing that has ever happened
to me. Annie and I both had nightmares for ages

afterwards. I still do, sometimes, and I think Annie does too, though she wouldn't admit it.

When we came to the edge of the woods that day, all scraped and scratched and doubled over with stitches, we found ourselves in the middle of a housing estate. I don't think either of us could have run any further. Annie had ricked her ankle and was hobbling badly, and now that we had stopped I could feel my cuts throbbing, making me feel sick.

We managed to stagger to the nearest house and ring the bell. It was an old lady who answered the door. I was just so relieved that she was old! She looked a bit like my gran. She was horrified when she saw the state we were in. We tried to tell her what had happened, but Annie was sobbing too much and I was shaking so violently I could hardly speak.

In the end I just begged to be allowed to ring my mum;
but even then, when I heard Mum's voice, all I could do
was weep. The old lady had to take the phone from me
and tell Mum where we were. Then Annie rang home
and Rachel was there, and I heard her screaming down
the phone.

"Where are you? Where have you been? I've been
going crazy! We've called the police!"

After that, it is all a bit of a blur. Mum arrived in a
cab, and Rachel's mum in her car, and Rachel in
the police car, and we had to tell the police
the whole story. We had to do it in front of
our mums. That was almost the worst
part. The old lady said she knew the
cottage where we had been; she said it
had stood empty for months. It was
empty when the police went round to
investigate. The woman who
had pretended to be Harriet
had disappeared. But she had
left a note which said, I AM
SO SORRY. My bag was
still there, though not
my mobile.

The police told us that they'd put a trace on the phone, but she must have dumped it somewhere 'cos it's never turned up. Ages afterwards, Annie came across the number written on a scrap of paper in her purse. "Megan's mobile". She wanted me to try ringing it, just to see, but I wouldn't; I would have been too scared, in case anyone answered. I told Annie that she ought to throw it away.

"We don't want to keep being reminded!"

It was like with my bag. It still had all my stuff in it, but I just couldn't even bear to touch it, it was like it had been contaminated, like diseased fingers had pawed and palped at it, so Mum emptied everything out and put the bag in the dustbin. I said to Annie that she should do the same with my mobile phone number.

There was a time when Annie would have argued, or even rung the number herself, but sometimes, these days, she actually listens to what I say. Sometimes she even does what I tell her! Which is what she did on this occasion.

"I 'spect you're probably right," she said. And lo and behold, she screwed up the paper and tossed it into the bin. I felt a whole lot better once she'd done that. Even if the phone did turn up one day, I couldn't ever bring myself to use it again.

Another thing the police did was take Annie's computer away. I don't know exactly what they do when they take computers away, but I think they were hoping to find out who it was that Annie was talking to in the chatroom. I mean, it was obviously the same person that was pretending to be Harriet Chance pretending to be Harriet's daughter Lori, but what they wanted to know was: *who was this person*?

Me and Annie both had to go to the police station, with our mums, and look through all these photographs in the hope that one of them would turn out to be her. The woman. We looked and looked as hard as we could, until our eyes started aching with the strain of it, but there wasn't any photograph that was even the least little bit like. I felt quite guilty that we couldn't be more helpful. There was this nice policewoman who told us to take our time and not to worry if we couldn't identify anybody, but I felt that we had behaved so stupidly, and put everyone to so much trouble, not to mention upsetting our mums, and Annie's dad, and Rachel, that I really would have liked to be able to point my finger and say "That one!" But in the end I couldn't, and neither could Annie.

We couldn't even be helpful about the car. All we could remember for sure was that it was red. So then we had to look at pictures of cars, and Annie thought it was a VW and I thought it was a Ford, and neither of us had noticed the number at all. Not even just one digit. Not even a letter! But I remembered the name "Jan" in the books, and "Love from Mummy," and then a bit later I remembered how one of the books had had the words "Janis Patmore: her book" written in it. I told Mum, and Mum said we must tell the police immediately. It turned out to be the clue that they needed, 'cos they actually managed to trace the woman. She hadn't really bothered to cover her tracks, so once they'd got the name it was quite easy. Maybe – this was what Mum said – she secretly wanted to be caught. "To stop her doing to anyone else what she did to you."

She obviously felt bad about it, or she wouldn't have left the note saying sorry. And what the police discovered was really sad. Janis Patmore had been the woman's daughter, her only daughter, and just a few months ago she had been killed in a terrible motor accident. She had only been twelve years old, and Harriet Chance had been her favourite author, just like she is mine.

The police said they thought the woman's brain had got muddled by grief, and that she had gone into the chatroom hoping to find her lost daughter – and instead, through Annie, she had found me. With one part of her brain, the muddled part, she might actually have thought that I *was* her daughter. But with the other part she would have known that I wasn't; which was why, at the end, she had come to her senses and shouted at us to go. It was like she had suddenly woken up to the truth and realised what she was doing.

When Mum heard this she said, "That is so tragic! The woman needs help, not punishment." The police assured us that she was getting help, and Mum said "Thank goodness. I know that what she did was terribly wrong, but she was obviously beside herself." And then she said, "That poor woman!"

I was somewhat indignant, at first. I mean, that poor woman had given me and Annie the worst fright either of us had ever had; and as I said to Mum, "Suppose she hadn't let us go?"

Mum said, "Then I would probably have ended up every bit as distraught and disturbed as that poor soul." She said that losing a child was just about the worst thing that could happen to a parent, and I knew that I should feel sorry for the woman, and I do try to, thought it is not easy. Mum says that when I'm older I will be more understanding. At the moment, it is still too close and I still get too scared. But sometimes I find myself remembering how the woman spoke on the answerphone, saying "Darling, where are you?" and "Please speak to me" and then I do, genuinely, feel sorry for her and think that maybe one day I shall be able to forgive her.

In the meantime, our story has been all over the papers, and on the radio and TV. It has been so embarrassing and horrible! I have felt all the time that everyone is looking at me and going, "That is the girl who was so stupid and has caused so much trouble." For ages I didn't want to go out for fear of being stared at. Annie felt the same. She always used to say that when she grew up she wanted to be a celeb, but I think she has changed her mind. She says that being famous is no fun and she would just like to be plain Annabel Watson that no one has ever heard of.

Our mums, I must say, were not very sympathetic. They were right at the beginning, but once they had got over the first shock, and the relief at having us back, they became a bit stern and told us that we had brought it all on ourselves. Mum did say that at least if other children could learn from our mistakes it would be one good thing to come out of "the whole sorry episode". She said, "You have both got off very lightly, and if a little bit of embarrassment is the price you have to pay, so be it."

I couldn't really argue with her. Even now when I think what *could* have happened, I get so tied up inside that I have to immediately start doing multiplication tables very quickly in my head, or gabbling nonsense like Mary-had-a-little-lamb, its-fleece-was-white-as-snow-as-snow-as-snow, until the knots have untied and the panic has stopped.

Before that terrible day, I don't think, probably, that many people at school knew who we were. We were just nonentities. Now – unfortunately – we are known throughout the school. We've had visits from the police, we've had lectures from teachers, we've even had a talk from Mrs Gibson in morning assembly, everybody from Year Seven to the Sixth Form, warning us about the dangers of meeting strangers from chatrooms. Mrs Gibson didn't actually mention me and Annie by name, but by then we'd been in the papers, so she didn't have to. Everybody knew. Heads turned, all over the hall. People around us started whispering. In the playground at break we could feel that we were being pointed at and talked about.

Most of the people in our class were really nice and said that what had happened could just as easily have happened to any of them – "We can all make mistakes!" But one or two said how dumb could you get, and one girl, Rozalie Dunkin, even blamed us for the fact that her parents had now taken her computer away and would only let her use it under supervision. She said it was so unfair.

"I'd never do anything that stupid!"

Me and Annie hung our heads, not knowing what to say, but another girl came to our rescue. Katie Purvis. (Who we are now really good friends with.) Katie pointed out that *at the time* you don't always realise you're being stupid.

"If you realised, you wouldn't do it."

Rozalie just tossed her head and said, "*I'd* realise. I'm not an idiot! Now we've got to put up with all these boring lectures."

Fortunately, not everyone thought they were boring, but Annie and me did feel quite bad about it.

We've both had to go for counselling (though not together). We've had to talk about what happened, and say how we feel. I didn't want to, at first. I didn't even want to think about it, but you can't always choose what you're going to think about. Thoughts pop into your brain when you are least expecting them. So in the end I started talking, telling it all over again, though I'd already been through it with Mum, and the police. And after a while it started to get easier, so that I now feel a bit better than I did. But I know that it will always be with me, and that I will never again do anything so foolish, not if I live to be a hundred.

Annie and I never really talk about that day. I think we are both too ashamed, and also it was just too scary. It scared me so much that I stopped nagging Mum to let me go into chatrooms. I even stopped nagging at her to let me have a computer. I thought Mum would be pleased. I thought she would say, "Well, at least you have learnt your lesson!" I couldn't really blame her if that's what she'd said. I'm all Mum's got in the world, and she might have lost me. She'd already told me that it made her blood run cold to think what might have happened.

"You're so precious to me, Megan!"

I said, "You're precious to me, Mum! That's why I don't care any more if we don't have a computer. I don't want one!"

You'll never guess what Mum said? In this very brisk tone of voice she said, "Well, that's where I beg to differ. *I* think we need to get you one as soon as possible, so that you can learn to use it properly and responsibly, without putting yourself at risk."

Anxiously I said, "But I don't ever want to go into a chatroom!" To which Mum said, "Nonsense! Of course you'll go into chatrooms. But you'll do it with me, and you'll stick to the rules. I don't want you growing up not knowing how to take care of yourself!"

Well. There are times when Mum can really surprise me. I thought she'd be so angry she'd never trust me ever again. But she said that in some ways she blamed herself.

"I've kept you too wrapped up in cotton wool."

At the time when she said it, when I was still feeling all shaky and terribly, horribly scared, I thought to myself that I liked being wrapped up in cotton wool. I didn't ever want to be unwrapped! But Mum says you can't live in a cocoon for ever, and I expect she is right. I am beginning to come out of it a bit now.

Annie has almost gone back to being her old bouncy self, which for a long while she wasn't. I hated seeing Annie all meek and subdued. I was quite relieved when she said to me one day that it might be fun to visit the joke shop in the shopping centre and buy some pretend scabs to stick on ourselves.

"Really gruesome ones... and grollies! You can buy grollies, all green and yucky!"

I knew then that she was still the same old Annie. We did go to the joke shop and buy scabs – and grollies, and some boils-on-the-point-of-bursting – but I said I didn't think we ought to wear them to school. I mean, we were in enough trouble as it was. For once, Annie agreed with me. Wonders will never cease! But like I said, Annie does now actually listen to me occasionally. Sometimes. Just now and again. If she always did *everything* I told her, I would know there was something seriously wrong.

Annie's mum was really across with her that day. Once she'd stopped hugging her, and crying, that is. Both our mums hugged and cried. Even Rachel did. But afterwards, Annie's mum told her that she should have known better. She had been warned over and over about going to meet people from chatrooms. Annie sobbed and said that she had thought it would be all right, because it was a woman, but her mum said that didn't make any difference.

"Besides, how did you know that it was a woman? It could have been a man. It could have been anyone!"

Rachel said, "It *was* anyone."

It certainly wasn't Harriet Chance. One of the horridest things is that for a while I thought I wouldn't ever want to read a Harriet Chance book again. I couldn't bear to see them all, in my bedroom! It was like I was muddling the real Harriet with the pretend one. It gave me a sick feeling in my stomach. But then something wonderful occurred. Caroline, Harriet's editor, rang up and said that Harriet was very upset about somebody impersonating her, and the terrible time that we'd had, and she wanted to do something to make up for it. She'd suggested that perhaps she might visit our school and talk to all of Year Seven about her books, and how she wrote them. And Mrs Gibson agreed! She said, "You've had all the lectures. Now it's time to move on."

Harriet came last week. I was really on tenterhooks, wondering what she would be like, and how I would feel. I kept thinking, what would I do if she walked into the library and it was *her*? The one that had pretended. What if she hadn't pretended? What if it had been the real Harriet all along?

Well, but it wasn't. That was just my fevered brain. The woman who came into the library was as different as could be from that other one. She was just as I had always imagined her. Small, and slim, and friendly, with mouscy hair – a bit limp, but not grey – and rather quiet and shy. But really, really nice!

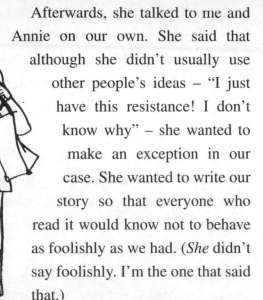

Afterwards, she talked to me and Annie on our own. She said that although she didn't usually use other people's ideas – "I just have this resistance! I don't know why" – she wanted to make an exception in our case. She wanted to write our story so that everyone who read it would know not to behave as foolishly as we had. (*She* didn't say foolishly. I'm the one that said that.)

"Is that all right?" she asked. "Would you mind?"

Annie and I just blushed and beamed and said we thought that would be really neat.

"And naturally," she said, "I'll dedicate it to you both."

So we really will have a book with our names inside! Mum says it is more than we deserve. Annie's mum says that what Harriet ought to put is "To Megan, who was led astray by her very stupid friend".

Poor Annie! It is so unfair. She feels extra bad about it, since she was the one who arranged it all.

190

"It was supposed to be your birthday treat!"

But I don't blame Annie. I was just as much in the wrong as she was. I have told her this.

"I know you *suggested* it, but I didn't have to agree."

She thought that I would hate her, but of course I don't. How could I hate Annie? Especially after all we have been through together. She's my best friend! My very *very* best friend.

She always will be.